ATTY IN LOVE

TIM LOCKETTE

SEVEN STORIES PRESS
NEW YORK • OAKLAND • LONDON

A TRIANGLE SQUARE BOOK FOR YOUNG READERS
PUBLISHED BY SEVEN STORIES PRESS

SEVEN STORIES PRESS
140 Watts Street
New York, NY 10013
www.sevenstories.com

Teachers may order free examination copies of Seven Stories Press titles.
Visit https://www.sevenstories.com/pg/resources-academics
or email academic@sevenstories.com.

Library of Congress Cataloging-in-Publication Data

Names: Lockette, Tim, author.
Title: Atty in love / Tim Lockette.
Description: New York : Seven Stories Press, 2024. | "A Triangle Square book for young readers." | Audience: Ages 10-14 years. | Audience: Grades 7-9. | Summary: Thirteen-year-old Atty falls for Emory Mumbford at the county fair, but when she learns his family owns Emily, the captive elephant she wants to free, she is torn between her emotions and her commitment to animal freedom.
Identifiers: LCCN 2024003346 | ISBN 9781644213988 (hardcover) | ISBN 9781644213995 (ebook)
Subjects: CYAC: Animal rights--Fiction. | Elephants--Fiction. | Interpersonal relations--Fiction. | Multiracial people--Fiction. | LCGFT: Novels.
Classification: LCC PZ7.1.L6233 Av 2024 | DDC [Fic]--dc23
LC record available at https://lccn.loc.gov/2024003346

Book design by Jon Gilbert

Printed in the USA.

9 8 7 6 5 4 3 2 1

For Buffy

CHAPTER ONE

◇

I've lived in Alabama for my whole life, minus a few days in Florida, but I'm not very good at being Southern.

Football bores me. I've never called Dad "sir," and I don't think I could do it without laughing. I don't have any opinions about barbecue. If you don't eat meat, barbecue is just a sauce. Ketchup, vinegar, and sugar, that's all. People who get a mouthful of barbecue and shake their heads and lift their hands like they're getting the Holy Spirit—I'm not saying they're faking, but if I reacted to barbecue sauce that way, I'd be faking. And if I shook my head and lifted my hands because of the Holy Spirit, that would be fake, too.

I know these are things that Southerners are supposed to do, because I see these posts online all the time. "Twelve Movies All Southern Girls Love." "Why Southern Girls Have to Get Everything Monogrammed." "Five Romantic Plantation Houses Any Southern Girl Would Want to Get Married In." Apparently Instagram knows I'm Southern, and a girl, and white. But there's a lot it doesn't know, like the fact that I've just now turned thirteen—old enough to officially be on Instagram—even though I've been on the app for years. And, apparently, a lot of people on Instagram don't know what went down on plantations.

But there's one Southern thing I can reach out and touch, something I know is real. The blues. Not the music so much, but the life the music is about. People on Instagram are always saying that this thing or that thing is a "whole mood," but the blues is the only mood I know whole.

The blues killed my mom, you know. My mom, who was even worse than me at being Southern. My mom, who was laughed at for wearing a Starfleet uniform to church. My mom, who people whispered about when she walked down the streets of Houmahatchee. My mom, who wrote a brilliant, unpublished book about faster-than-light travel in popular culture.

"The hope at the heart of modern science fiction is based on a technology that, according to physics, will never exist," she says in the book's first chapter.

I never really knew my mom, but as I get older, I seem to become more and more like her. I'm someone people whisper about. People recognize me in the aisles of Walmart. *That's her, the dog lawyer girl,* they say. I spend all my free time on a big writing project that no one seems to understand. (In my book bag right now: The Alabama Constitution of 1901 and *Nonprofit Grant Writing for Beginners.*)

There are moments when I'm sure I'm thinking thoughts that my mother thought before. It's not just a feeling. My mom wrote a lot of papers and articles about science fiction, and whenever I pick one up, I see someone like me staring back.

"Science has not unwoven the rainbow," she wrote. "The stars are more beautiful because we know what they are. When we look in the sky, we're seeing into the depth of space and the beginning of Time."

Like my mom, I get that chilly feeling that comes from knowing the stars are all balls of gas that will one day burn out. All the puppies and kittens and toddlers holding their teddy bears will be gone one day, and the universe won't care.

It's not on my mind all the time, but the stars do come out every night, you know.

And I know, too, that if you have a relative who's committed suicide, you're more likely to do it yourself. So there's that, looming over my head.

"I'll never get out of these blues alive," I said to Taleesa, my stepmom, one night as we cleaned the kitchen. When depression hits me—that feeling like I'm on a planet with too-strong gravity—it's usually after dinner.

"That's the title of a song, you know," Taleesa told me.

I chuckled darkly. "Sounds like an awful song," I said. "Someone's even whinier than me."

Taleesa shook her head. "No, no, no. A very popular song. John Lee Hooker. A king of the blues, if you like that sort of thing," she said.

Taleesa's no blues fan, but her father was. We call him Old Martinez, because my brother Martinez was named after him. He never lived in Houmahatchee, but he's another one of the ghosts who float over our house. I saw him only once: a proud-looking old man with a shiny lapel pin, lying in a casket in a cold church in Milwaukee.

To me, Old Martinez is like George Washington—familiar and at the same time impossibly ancient and foreign. Taleesa lets only a little bit of his story slip out now and then. How he got arrested in a riot in the 1960s, just because he was there, and because he was Black. The dozens of jobs he worked, driving a bus, sweeping the floor in a factory. How he would shovel snow off the roof of their house in the winter to keep it from collapsing. It's hard to believe that snow has that much weight. I mean, it's just little floaty flakes, isn't it? It's also kind of hard to believe that Old Martinez is so closely related to my brother Martinez, who loves air conditioning, lives entirely inside video games, and can't start a lawn mower without help.

"Old Martinez, he loved John Lee Hooker," Taleesa said. "Well, maybe loved isn't the right word. He listened to him all the time. Does a smoker love cigarettes, or is it just a habit? I never really understood the appeal. Life is hard enough without singing about how depressed you are."

That perked me up. "You think Old Martinez had depression, too?"

"No," Taleesa said matter-of-factly. "He didn't have the flu, either. Or food poisoning, or any of that. Some people don't have the money to go to the doctor, so they never have a name for what they've got. They're just sick, and they miss work, and they hope they don't die. A lot of men would rather die than talk about their feelings, and a lot of them do die."

Taleesa is tough. She tolerates my moodiness, but only just. Sometimes, I have to admit, I feel like she's kind of cold about it.

"So Old Martinez didn't have time to talk about his feelings," I said. "But he did listen to this guy, John Lee Hooker, who sang about the blues."

"Only in the car," Taleesa said. "Always in the car, he had a whole rack of blues tapes. I suppose I still have them, out in the tool shed somewhere."

After that, I had to hear this song. *Out of these blues alive.* I guess I could have just looked it up on my phone, but for some reason I wanted to hear the song as *he* heard it. So I braved the dark and the spiders and went out with a flashlight and dug around in our tool shed. I hit the jackpot: a fake leather case full of old-timey cassette tapes. Some were clear plastic, with the names of the singers almost completely rubbed off. Others were dubbed copies, with JOHN LEE written on them in Old Martinez's surprising handwriting: neat, bubbly-shaped letters. My handwriting is skinny and messy like an old man's; my step-grandfather wrote neatly the way a girl in middle school is supposed to. I also found an old boom box, without the power cord, and I emptied all the flashlights in the house to get enough batteries to power it.

Alone in my room with the boom box on my lap, I started one of the tapes. At first, I thought the boom box was broken, because for a long time, there was nothing but a tiny sound of tapping on a cymbal. Then there's the voice of an old man saying *never never.* Again and again. He'll never get out of these blues. Not if he lives to a hundred.

That voice sounds a lot like what I imagine Old Martinez would have sounded like. But usually, when old people say stuff, they sound so convinced, like they only talk about things they know for sure. John Lee Hooker sounds different. You can almost hear him shaking his head as he says he doesn't understand why he has the blues. He genuinely doesn't know. He just knows that he's up all night, that the same thing is on the radio every time he turns it on, and that nothing ever seems to change.

There it was. Another person in the world who knew what it was like to be me. I guess it's not just me who's up all night, thinking too much. I had to hear more. I listened to John Lee Hooker's whole story, as told on this tape. His true love died, but he visited her grave every Decoration Day. The Motor City was burning, and he didn't know what to do.

Where had this music been all my life? I'd heard country and bluegrass and Atlanta rappers who wanted to make it rain. None of it said anything about my life. But this simple *tick tick tick* of the drum, this one guy growling about being doomed with the blues—was something I could understand.

Toni, my therapist, says she gets mad when she hears people talking about depression as "the blues." Depression is a disease, she says, and the blues is a mood.

Taleesa says you have to be careful about claiming blues music for yourself. A lot of Black people see it as music that's full of life, she says. Taleesa says this music is realistic about problems that Black people and poor people and maybe nearly all people face. There's a difference, she says, between visiting your wife's grave every Decoration Day and just *feeling* like you're in a graveyard on Decoration Day.

But John Lee Hooker says *If I live to be a hundred, I never will.* Whatever condition it is that he's got, I've got it too, or something like it. There's something inside of me that no one explains better than John Lee Hooker.

So I stole my brother's drumsticks. This was the year Martinez got into sixth-grade band. He didn't seem to have any great passion for music, but as he's gotten older and taller, grownups have started pestering him about whether he's going to play ball in high school. One day he asked what he could do to get out of this football thing forever, and that landed him behind a snare drum going *rum-pa-pum-pum* in the sixth grade Christmas concert. He hardly ever practices his drums at home, so I figured he wouldn't mind if I snuck into his room and snatched the sticks off his music stand.

I put on headphones and tapped on the frame of my bed, drumming along with John Lee Hooker. *Cain't nobody tell me, just exactly why,* John Lee sang. Soon Taleesa had to buy me my own set of drumsticks, because I was drumming on the bed every time I was bored, or down, or worried about things that a lot of other people don't seem to worry much about.

Things like the fate of the stars and the planets. Things like the idea of living to one hundred and being depressed the entire time. Things like making a presentation to the Strudwick County Commission.

▮ ▮ ▮

I have a sturdy wooden box that I use whenever I have to give a speech in a public place. It has a warm brown finish to it, and little handles cut out in the sides, to make it easier to carry. If I have something to bring to the podium—a hundred-page report, printed photos of dogs and cats, notes on little cards—I carry them in the box. Then when I'm called up to speak, I carefully place all the items from the box on the podium. Then I turn the box over, put it on the floor, and stand on it so I'm the same height as the grownups I'm talking to.

Sometimes it gets a little laugh from the audience and warms them up. Some people never laugh. Some people just aren't all that warm. As I looked out on the Strudwick County Commission, I couldn't see any of the commissioners laughing.

"Before you even start, Miss Peale," County Commission Chairman Broderick Hegarty said, "let me just say how delighted I am to see a pretty young lady like yourself taking an interest in public policy."

Pretty. Did you hear that? Almost nobody calls me pretty in real life. But lately, "pretty lady" has started popping up when official-types want to talk down to me. They used to say "little girl," but over the last school year that started changing.

Lots of things are changing, in fact. Changes nobody asked for, particularly me. I'd gladly skip the teen years and go directly to being a grown lady, even an old lady. But now I'm thirteen and I'm not a girl or an old lady. I'm more like a transporter accident from *Star Trek.* Or maybe a better example is *Manimal,* that old TV show that Martinez pulls up sometimes on his phone. *Manimal* is about a classy British guy in a tux who occasionally turns into a panther or a hawk or some other animal. I guess he fights evil and solves crime, but what the show is really about is the transformation: every episode has these long, gross sequences in which Manimal gets all rubbery-faced and screams in pain while his skin roils and bubbles like soup on a pot. That's what being a teenager is like. It's supposed to be a thrilling adventure, but in fact you spend most of the time looking in horror at your bubbling skin while Martinez laughs at your pain.

All these changes are things I don't like to talk about in detail, even with Toni, my therapist. When something happens to my body that I need to discuss with Taleesa, we typically talk about it in a Popeye voice or pirate-speak, which somehow makes it a little easier.

Still, bubbling skin or not, I have work to do. That's why I was standing there, in front of the commission. Talking to judges and county commissioners is hard. They're always sitting down, up on a big platform, and you're always looking up at them trying to speak clearly into the microphone, with a bunch of people in the audience behind you.

"So, gentlemen," I said to the commissioners. "It's clear that Strudwick County has a problem. A stray animal problem. I realize we're a small town and a lot of people don't mind letting dogs run free, but as more people and more animals live here, it's beginning to become an issue. Commissioner Hegarty, I hear that when you took those Korean businessmen for a tour of town, there was a pack of wild dogs wandering around downtown Houmahatchee. We all know about the All-Day-Singing Incident."

"I'm sorry?" said one of the commissioners. "The singing incident? I don't know about that."

Hegarty cleared his throat. "She's taking about the thing at Emmaus Church. They were having a singing and dinner on the ground, and they left all the covered dishes out on the table outside. A bunch of stray dogs got to them."

"I have heard about that," the commissioner said. "And this is our concern how? How's it on the county's radar?"

Troy Butler stood up in the back of the room. I keep wanting to call him Deputy Troy Butler, but he's Sheriff Troy now. Sheriff is a position you have to run for, like mayor, and I imagine it's easy to get elected to anything when you have a dimple in your chin and arm muscles that are just the right size. A lot of ladies said they'd vote for him twice if they could.

"As you know, gentlemen, just about anything that happens in the county generates a call to the Sheriff's Office," Troy said. "In this case, some guns were brought out, there was some talk of running around the neighborhood to get the dogs, which the neighbors didn't particularly care for, and ultimately a deputy had to kind of talk the church members into a consensus. Nobody got hurt, though we did arrest a deacon on weapons charges."

"I heard about that," the commissioner said. "I still don't understand that arrest. If a church is private property and they don't object to guns, what's wrong with a member carrying a concealed pistol? Even if he doesn't have a permit?"

"It wasn't a concealed carry arrest," Butler said. "The deacon's an ex-felon. He's served his time but he's not allowed to own a gun."

Am I the only person in the room who thinks it's weird that so many people bring their guns to church? I looked around. In front of me, I saw the five commissioners, looking very bored. Behind me, on wooden pews that were obviously salvaged from a church, sat a handful of other guys, a bit younger and pudgier, in polo shirts, looking at their phones—guys who worked for the county, counting money or running the street department. There was Sheriff Butler standing up in the back, and at a table to my right sat Backsley Graddoch, the county attorney, in his suit and looking, as always, like someone way too rich to live in Strudwick County. All of them had an I-need-coffee glaze over their eyes. Yes, I was the only person in the room who thought it was strange to bring guns to church.

"So," I said. "As you see, we have a problem. Y'all all probably know I see the problem differently than some of you. Some people say there are too many dogs. I say there are too few families that can adopt a dog. But here's the thing: as it turns out, the best solution to our problem is one that we can all agree on. With a long-term plan to put animals and families together, we can cut down on our stray population and also cut down, and eventually eliminate, the need to put animals to sleep. Other communities have done this. Not a lot, but some. We're poor compared to some of those counties, but we can do this. We can be a trailblazer."

This was the inspiring part of my speech. I don't talk like that normally, but I'd written it on notecards and practiced it so much I didn't even need the cards.

I paused for effect, and to look at each of the commissioners to see if they looked inspired. They looked like people who hadn't been inspired in a long time. I went on.

"I'm not asking you to spend any money," I said. "At least, not this year. Not much money in the future. Volunteers will do most of the work. What I'm asking is for you to approve this plan. Make it your official plan. That will help us get attention and will help us when we go to people who can give us money."

Just so you'll know: as I said this, each of the commissioners sat there with my no-kill-shelter plan in their hands. It's about a hundred pages of stuff, which I researched and wrote entirely myself. The plan starts with the Strudwick County Animal Shelter announcing its goal to become the first no-kill shelter in a high-poverty area within the next twenty years. With the attention we get from that announcement, we go to big charities and ask them for money to help with our goal. Then we set up partnerships with adoption agencies in other cities so people in, say, Atlanta, can adopt our extra dogs. And we set up something we've never had here—a foster care network where people take some dogs and cats home temporarily when the shelter is too full.

I could see, as the commissioners flipped through the plan, that some of them were just looking at it now for the first time. I'd sent it to them a week before. I saw a couple of them looking surprised.

"I'm curious," said one of the commissioners, a guy named Frank Feeney. "Who wrote this?"

That question kind of surprised me. "Well, like I said, I wrote it," I said.

Commissioner Feeney looked at me with a kind of glaze in his eye.

"No, I mean, who wrote it originally?" he said.

I put my hands on my hips. It's one of those things Dad always tells me not to do in a courtroom. Not before a judge. It looks defiant. But I was offended.

"I assure you, I'm small, but I'm plenty capable of writing a 100-page legal document," I said.

"She's the real deal, gentlemen," said Backsley Graddoch, the county attorney. "I don't agree with her on most things, but I can tell you she's a real legal draftsman."

"Well, that doesn't make any sense," Commissioner Feeney said. "I thought all these bills, all these proclamations . . . don't they all come first from some kind of lobbyist or some kind of activist, and then you rewrite them, Backsley, and then they come to us? I mean, a person can't just, I mean, *write a plan* and bring it to us . . . right?"

Everybody was quiet for a moment. A couple of the commissioners looked at each other like they were about to burst out laughing. Finally, Backsley Graddoch spoke up.

"Commissioner, I think that's exactly where we are right now," he said. "This young lady is an activist and she's brought you a plan. I think that's fair to say, isn't it, Miss Peale, that you're an activist?"

"Sure," I said. "I mean, I'm a citizen. I want my government to do something. So I wrote a plan and brought it to you."

Commissioner Feeney shook his head.

"But who do you *work* for?" he said.

"I don't work for anybody," I said. I was starting to get worked up a bit. "I live here. I'm a citizen asking something from my government."

"Frank," said Commissioner Hegarty, "I think you're overcomplicating this. Let's just move on and I'll explain it to you later."

I held up my hand. "With all due respect," I said. "I hope that 'move on' includes some kind of motion to adopt the plan."

Hegarty made a quick frowny-face, just for a second, that let me know he was uncomfortable being put on the spot.

"Here's what I think we should do," he said. "Let's let Mr. Graddoch, our attorney, have a go at this. He's learned in the law and he knows what our interests are. Miss Peale, how about you and Mr. Graddoch work together and make sure we have a plan we can pass?"

I tried not to show it, but I really wanted to roll my eyes. It's always ten steps forward and nine steps back. I've already written a plan. I know exactly what I want to do. I could explain it if people would just let me. But now I have to sit down with my biggest rival and do all that work again.

"I'm more than happy to work with Miss Peale," Graddoch said. "But I think I should note from the outset that there may not be a lot we can do. As you know, the Alabama Constitution limits the powers of the County Commission considerably . . ."

"I've taken that into consideration, actually," I said. "If you'd just let me present the plan, you'll see—"

"I second the motion," Frank Feeney said. "Let the two of them work together and come back to us."

And just like that, by a vote of five to zero, I'm back to the drawing board. Rewriting my plan.

■ ■ ■

So, welcome to my world. I'm Atticus T. Peale, advocate for animals.

I got my start, and got mildly famous, by going to court and trying to save a dog that was set to be put to sleep. I won that case, more or less, which is why when I stand before the county commission I have to pick little bits of white-and-black dog hair off my dress. It's why, when I go to school, I worry a little about smelling like dog. And it's why, as I write this right now, I know my dog Easy is making a little warm spot in the front hallway of my house, curled up and watching the front door and waiting for me to come in.

When I come home from school or the animal shelter, I throw my book bag next to the coffee table and plop down on the couch and Easy jumps up on the couch and puts his warm head in my lap, knowing I'll pet him. And he always lets out a big heavy sigh just then, as if he'd been holding his breath all day waiting for me.

Sometimes I let out a big heavy sigh, too. Because after my first courtroom victory—saving Easy from death—my life as an activist or whatever I am hasn't gotten any easier. Since then I've been snookered by a governor, stalked by online trolls, actually shot at by a murderer, and examined by all kinds of social workers and counselors who seem convinced I'll explode and spatter them with purple ecto-plasm or something if they say something too wrong, or too triggery.

By the way, maybe we should rethink this phrase, "trigger warning." Did they really think about gunshot victims before they came up with that?

I did help my brother save an innocent man from going to prison, so that was cool. I've learned defending a human is a lot harder than defending an animal. Everyone believes you when you say an animal is innocent, but when police accused Jethro Gersham of killing a pawn shop owner in

Houmahatchee, most people just shook their heads and said they never knew Jethro had it in him. Everyone in town knew him, and they'd known him for years, but only a few of us questioned whether he really did it. Or maybe they did question the charges, but they reacted the same way they often react to innocent animals being put to sleep: a sad feeling, a shrug, and a sense that they can't really do anything about it.

Well, Martinez and I did something about it. Martinez was convinced from the beginning that Jethro was set up, and he was right: Gary Dudley, the pawn shop owner's business partner, committed the murder, and he made it look like Jethro was the shooter. My little brother unwound a mystery that had fooled the cops and almost every grownup in Houmahatchee, but sometimes it's easy to figure things out if you're just willing to believe in someone's innocence. Martinez believed in Jethro more than anybody, and he did most of the work. I got most of the credit, though, because I'm the one Gary Dudley tried to kill after we started raising questions about the crime.

Anyway, that's the sort of stuff I do in my free time.

I also write the weekly "Shelter Dogs" column in *The Houmahatchee Herald*, where I post photos and stories about dogs and cats waiting at the shelter, and I do keep a scrapbook of all the animals that were adopted by people who say they read about that animal in the newspaper. So that's cool, too.

But the bigger picture just hasn't changed a whole lot. Strudwick County is still home to lots of people who can barely afford to feed themselves and keep the lights on, so adopting a pet from the shelter probably isn't the best option for them. A lot of people are helping strays the way they know how. They put out some food or some scraps for a passing cat when they can. They buy a puppy for five dollars out of the back of a car in the Walmart parking lot, because they're worried that someone will simply abandon the puppy if it isn't sold. I've learned that you can't always judge someone when you see a dog chained in the front yard, drinking from a hubcap, or sleeping in a rusted-out car. People are doing their best.

What we need, though, is a plan to do better. When people have to move, and their landlord won't allow dogs, sometimes they just set the dog free, because they don't know there's another option. Some people would get a cat spayed or neutered if they had the money, but it's not high on their to-do list and they don't know where to go for help. That's why you see strays everywhere in Strudwick County. You see dogs roaming, in packs of four or five, through the Houmahatchee town square or down by the outdoor basketball court at school. You see cats who live in a sewage drain and eat out of the dumpster behind Captain D's.

When those roaming animals bug people, maybe by messing up the farmer's market or snapping at kids outside a football game, the county sends someone out to catch them. And when animals don't have collars or tags, the death count begins for them as soon as they're caught. I can put a doggy face in the paper and post videos on Facebook and beg and plead for someone to adopt a dog, but if they don't get adopted, in goes the needle. Put to sleep.

The sad thing is that I'm pretty sure all of these dogs and cats used to be someone's pet. They just don't have tags or chips. Why? Because money, I guess. Tags and chips cost money. Farms may also have something to do with it. Strudwick County used to be all farms. Everybody grew peanuts or something called shade tobacco, which is a kind of tobacco you wrap cigars in. Today it's all pine trees and chicken houses, and all the trees and chickens belong to some big business somewhere. Almost nobody's a full-on farmer anymore, but a lot of people think farm rules still apply. A tough person, they think, ought to be able to slaughter a hog or pluck a chicken, which most people today have never done. So how can you cry and get all upset when your little dog goes off and doesn't come back?

I know all this farm stuff because people tell me. They stop me at Walmart and tell me how sweet it is what I'm doing and why it won't work but I sure am a smart, pretty girl. Twice I've argued with substitute teachers who told me my shelter work was a waste of time. One of them told me I should be working to help unborn children. That sounded bizarre to me, so I asked how the heck I'm supposed to help somebody who hasn't been born yet? Half the class looked at me in horror, like I'd pooped right there on the carpet.

So, anyway, my big plan was to put a stop to all this stray-animal chaos. Or at least put a stop to the last part of the story, where the needle goes in and the dog dies. I wrote a plan for how in twenty years—I'll be an old lady of thirty-three by then—we can have an animal shelter where not a single animal has to be put to sleep. It's not just *my* plan, it's *our* plan. I worked with Miss Megg, the director of the animal shelter, every step of the way.

In the first year, the plan was to start offering free spaying and neutering for people who can't afford to get their pets fixed. By year three, we wanted to have a partnership with Auburn University's veterinary school, where we pick up stray cats, get them fixed so they can't have babies, and just release them back into the wild if we can't find homes for them. By year five, we'd have a new set of county regulations to make sure people keep their dogs behind fences and their cats in the house. And all along, we'll keep up our work to attract rich folks from Atlanta and Mobile and Montgomery to come and adopt our pets.

Starting all that would take some money. I thought we should ask the county for money, but Miss Megg said you can't get blood from a turnip. She said we should ask big charities and the federal government for money instead. And to boost our chances of getting those grants, we should get Strudwick County and the City of Houmahatchee to sign off on our plans.

And that's all I was asking the county commission to do just read our plan and approve it. But they can't do that, or claim they can't, because of the Alabama Constitution. It's true that Alabama has some strange rules. County governments run jails and animal shelters and things like that, but they're not allowed to do a lot of new things without permission from the state. If you want to set up something like a recycling program, you have to get the Alabama Constitution changed, which usually means the whole state gets to vote on it. The Alabama Constitution is about eight hundred pages long at this point, and we don't do a lot of recycling.

"I suspect we'll be adding another amendment before

all this master-plan stuff of yours is through," Backsley Graddoch said to me as we left the commission chamber. "You'll be the first teenager to amend the state Constitution, I suspect."

"*Bleah*," I said.

"It would look good on a resume," Graddoch said. "There are young people in college right now, future law students, who'd kill to have the resume you have already."

"Double *bleah*," I said.

Graddoch shook his head. "I just don't understand you, Atty," he said. "We're very different people, I think. Why do you think it's so bad to claim some honor for yourself? It's okay to make a dollar as a lawyer. It's okay to become a senator or judge in the future if you work for it. I don't know why you're so allergic to . . . I don't know, whatever you're allergic to."

"To being a big shot?" I said. "I'll tell you why. I'll tell you what I hear in what you're saying. When you say people would kill for a good resume, I hear you talking about people who would kill. I hear you talking about people who want to look good. That's not what I'm about. I'm about helping animals. I want to be a normal person in a better world, not an important person in the world we have now."

▮ ▮ ▮

But maybe I would like to look good, really.

Not that I'd kill. But maybe I'd do some desperate things to look, well, better than I do.

Ever notice how people treat folks who are really good-looking? A big, burly guy works behind the counter at an auto-parts shop, but when a pretty lady comes in, he turns almost girly, with a bright, gentle smile. Or when Troy Butler comes around, and every woman's voice has a lilt in it. When you're good-looking, I think, life is like a musical. Everything is singsong. If you're dancing on a table, and you fall backward without even looking behind you, a bunch of handsome sailors will appear and gracefully catch you.

I'm not ugly, but I'm not dancing-on-the-table beautiful either. This is what I know in my brain. What you know in your heart is different. Sometimes I look in the mirror and it's just sad, sad the way it's sad when I hear my voice on tape. When I was ten, I was sure I'd grow up to look and sound like a British lady in a movie with a long slinky dress and a British accent and a cigarette on a long black stick, held in delicate gloved hands. But in the mirror I'm a troll doll with a toothbrush. In recordings I sound like a smart-alecky eight-year-old boy who likes to fish and hunt. Once time I told a grownup that Dad is not from Houmahatchee but in fact grew up in northern Alabama, almost in Tennessee. And she told me she could tell because I have an "Appalachian face." I don't even know what an Appalachian face is, but I know she didn't mean it as a compliment, and that hurts me more than anything any creepy old guy has said to me on the internet.

So in my heart, I feel ugly. But my brain has a different idea. Taleesa tells me I'm good-looking enough for her to worry about me and boys, and Taleesa doesn't tell lies. My bio-mom looks great in all her photos, even toward the end when she wasn't okay, and I think my Dad is reasonably handsome, too. Generally I think reasonably good-looking people have reasonably good-looking kids. And when I asked Reagan Royall which one of us was the hot friend, she didn't even pause for a second.

"Me of course," she said. "But it's not a fair comparison. I'm Elvis hot. Comely and dangerous. A moody musician from the backwoods with a crooked grin. But in any normal pair, you'd be the hot friend. You're wholesome hot. Well, hott*ish* and wholesome."

Coming from Reagan, that's a compliment. I know how to read her. She's determined to get through her teen years undamaged, like a boy in movies who steals cars and plays with switchblades. If she feels insecure, she boasts like a rapper: lots of stuff about how powerful she is and how rich she'll be.

Sometimes she lays it on so thick that people think everything she says is a joke, but there are also things she never jokes about. Last year, when we were assigned a personal essay, our English teacher gave this beautiful, impassioned speech about how a writing class was a perfect place to share our worries and shame and grief. Reagan responded that she shares those things only with her lord and savior Jesus Christ. She got sent to the office for being disrespectful to people of faith. It didn't take long for Mrs. St. Stephens to realize that Reagan was dead born-again serious, and the teacher had to apologize in front of the whole class.

Reagan is right about her level of hotness. She only wishes her smile was crooked like Elvis. But with her asymmetrical haircuts and vampire-biker wardrobe, she keeps getting looks from guys who are old enough to drive. On the rare times we go to football games, seniors from the visiting side always try to chat her up. She claims she strings them along just so she can watch the horrified looks on their faces when she springs the "I'm thirteen" thing.

"Look at them running back to the little bleachers," she'll say. "I'm just doing my part for the team. We're here to humiliate the other side. That's what football is all about, for us spectators, right?"

Reagan doesn't spare feelings, so if she says I'm somewhat hot, it stands to reason that I'm some kind of minor planet in the solar system of hotness. Maybe not an obvious planet like Jupiter but at least some sort of trans-Neptunian object that scientists will investigate one day. I shared this notion, in exactly those words, with Reagan one day.

"So what you're saying is that you're the Pluto of hotness," she said. "I don't think that's a very good metaphor. Pluto, the coldest planety-thing."

I'm discovering that there are lots of problems with being the Pluto of hotness. My eccentric orbit brings me close to other bodies only once every 238 years. I'm small enough to be a moon of Jupiter. And I'm starting to think that those are the only choices I have. To be captured by Reagan's gravity, forever the nerdy wingman, or to swing way out into the dark, unclassifiable and alone—an awkward valentine sailing through space, wearing a giant pink heart that nobody sees.

So I guess it's happening. I guess I'm finally getting interested in . . . you know. Not boys. Still not interested in boys. They're not hairy enough, and they're too hairy, all at the same time. For me, it's still grown men and grown women.

When we're out at a restaurant and I see a couple, her and him, and he's got his muscular arm around her and their faces are close, I'll admit that it's hard for me not to stare. I don't know if it's him or her I like, but I'd like to be one of them, just then. But I can put it out of my mind most of the time. I'm still a late bloomer, but sometimes I wake up early in the morning with a weird yearning that I can't quite attach to anything, and I know that blooming may happen whether I want it or not.

I guess I'm a late bloomer in a lot of other ways. I was later than other girls in getting my period. And I guess I was lucky in that it happened in the summer, while I was working at the animal shelter, surrounded by women. As far as I know, Martinez was the only boy working at the shelter that summer, and I'd say he showed up only about half as often as he did the year before, when we were both there under court order.

So when I came out of the bathroom at the shelter and told Miss Megg what had happened, she and all the other girls at the shelter made a big deal out of it. Megg gave me an unopened box of maxipads she bought for herself, which was weird, and everybody started telling painful, embarrassing stories about how they got their period the first time. They kind of made me feel guilty that it didn't happen while I was standing at the whiteboard doing an algebra problem in front of the whole class.

Miss Megg sat me down with a glimmer in her eye and gave me a very heartfelt speech about how I was now a woman with the greatest power in the world, the power to bring life into the world.

You know, it did feel kind of powerful. But I couldn't stop thinking about the fact that I'd still have to get a guy to help me make a baby if I wanted one, which didn't seem powerful at all. I hate asking people for help.

At the time, I couldn't off the top of my head think of a guy I'd like to have a baby with. Premsyl Svoboda seemed like the best option, even though I kind of hated him. He was the best option because he was smart and always talked in full sentences in an indoor voice, instead of shouting dumb stuff like "PURPLE DEVILS RULE!" the way every other boy (and man) in Houmahatchee did from time to time. But even having Premsyl's baby didn't seem all that appealing.

I mean, it's powerful to be able to make a baby, but then after that, you've got a baby. You have to take care of it, instead of doing other stuff that you need to do.

And I can't help but think of my mom. They say some women get really depressed after giving birth. I know my mom struggled with depression for years before I was born, but I can't help but wonder if it was childbirth that pushed her over the edge. I don't want to go there myself.

"There's a thing called survivor's guilt," Toni told me when I brought this up in therapy. "You feel bad for surviving something, even though it's not your fault. Keep in mind that your mother made her own decisions, and you certainly aren't at fault for her death."

"That's not it," I told her. "I didn't even really know her. I don't feel any guilt at all. I want to know what landmine she stepped on, so I don't step on it too."

I hate talking to people about my mother. Not with Toni

so much, but with other people. People don't know what to say, so they say stupid things, like that they don't understand how she could have done it or that she had so much to live for. Sure she did. But that question, what was she depressed *about*? It really gets me.

Let's face it. There's a lot of sadness in the world if you're brave enough to look. You and I will wink out and exist no more. Our fondest memories will vanish, like an erased videotape in the landfill. The sun will die eventually and maybe there won't be a human left after that to think human thoughts and have human feelings. That's pretty sad. I didn't make this world and my mom didn't either. I think that we should be proud that we hope and work as much as we do, instead of being ashamed that we get crushed by despair sometimes.

I know most people in Houmahatchee think God will save them, and maybe he will, but I don't see a lot of evidence he exists. Seems like a coin toss to me. And even if God saves your tape in his video library, what about all the animals? I've heard that the Pope said you can bring your dog to Heaven. But what about the others? What about the innocent bunny and the eagle that innocently ate the bunny? I want a massive Heaven teeming with every critter that ever lived on this planet or any other. When I find a religion that promises me that, maybe I'll believe the world isn't a sad place.

I think my mom killed herself because when you're sad in Houmahatchee, you have to be sad in secret. If you're sad and you don't know why, nobody here wants to hear it. They'll say you just need Jesus, which has to be tough to hear if you already have Jesus, if you're already going to church and doing the best you can to get right with God. Or they'll tell you that you don't have anything to be sad about, which may be true, but there you are, still sad. Or if you tell them you're sad about all the animals who are going to die or about the fact that we'll never travel faster than light, they'll just laugh at you and say "bless her heart."

But if you're sad about something, you have to talk about it. You have to have someone to talk to, someone who takes it seriously. One thing I've learned from therapy: the way people heal your trauma is by making a big deal out of it with some kind of ritual that's even weirder than the trauma itself. Like all the picture-taking and hand-holding I got from the cops after Gary Dudley tried to kill me. Or the way Miss Megg made such an event after my first period. Or the psychotherapy that I'm still in today.

"You've told me all about how Miss Megg reacted to your period," Toni told me in our next session. "But you didn't tell me how you felt."

Honestly, I didn't feel anything, much. It felt like my yearly nosebleed. I really do get a bloody nose exactly once a year, always on a beautiful day in spring. The doctor says it's because of an allergy to pollen. I never feel any pain. Usually I'm sitting there reading and blood starts dropping onto the page. It's strange, but what am I supposed to feel about that? Shaving my legs for the first time was a much bigger deal than getting my period. Here I am with a razor, like a grown lady who could be in a swimsuit ad, but I'm still just a kid who plays Crossy Paws and talks to a toy squirrel.

When I came out of the bathroom after that first shave,

I guess I did feel like a grownup for just a minute. Adulting can give you a little thrill for a minute, but I still feel like it's a raw deal in the end, because you aren't allowed to go back. My whole life I've heard Taleesa talking about how nice it is to get home and take your bra off. The first time I wore one myself, I totally got what she was talking about. So that night, when we were all in the living room, I was the one who said the bra thing first, and it made me feel really grown up—until Martinez started making puking noises and ruined the whole moment.

That's what growing up is like. You have one moment of pride, the first time you do something. And then you've got to wear this dumb thing your whole life.

CHAPTER TWO

◇

One thing I love about John Lee Hooker is that he's honest. I get really tired of grownups who lie to kids. Our old governor, Fischer King, for example. He would go all over the state saying we should clean up the libraries and take out all the books with gay people in them, because you're putting the idea of sexual immorality in the heads of children. Then, later, the news comes out that he's been cheating on his wife for years. I can see why people who cheat or drink or use drugs would want to hide it, but I don't understand why people can't just lie to their own kids, instead of preaching at everybody and talking about *this generation* and all that.

John Lee Hooker is up front about his bad habits. He sings about drinking black coffee and smoking cigarettes all night. He's not too worried about whether some kid will hear him and want to do the same. He leaves it up to us.

I can't smoke cigarettes and I really don't want to. I'm not in with the kids who could get me that kind of contraband.

But I can drink black coffee.

Like the blues, coffee is what Dad calls an "acquired taste." An acquired taste is something that's yucky but you learn to like it. Like all those seafood restaurants in Mobile. It smells like the fish died right there, and the grownups are drinking big glasses of beer that look for all the world like pee, but then for weeks afterward people talk about how much they loved it. They're proud that they learned how to like this stuff.

I guess I'm proud that I take my coffee black. Taleesa lets me take the first cup if I fill the coffeemaker at night. It's set to come on at 5 a.m., and so am I. Up at five, walk Easy, then coffee. If you get up early once to work on something, your dog will hold you to it for the rest of your life. Time to get up, time for a walk.

I get up early to work on The Plan. It's a little easier now that Coach Chambliss has excused me from attending Alabama History class, which I have in first period. I can work on The Plan as a form of independent study as long as I take all the tests in History and pass them. It's really what's best for everybody. History with Coach Chambliss was a battle every day and it made my arm muscles sore because I always had my hand up.

They even let me go down to the County Administration Building sometimes, to work with Backsley Graddoch.

"I don't know about this skipping-Alabama-History thing," Graddoch would say. "How's a child going to learn about the Cassette Girls and all that other important stuff?"

I know Graddoch well enough now to recognize when he's joking, and it turns out that he's joking a great deal of the time. I think he really should wink when he makes fun of something like the Cassette Girls, because a lot of people might hear him and think he's serious.

The Cassette Girls were a bunch of women who got shipped down to Mobile to marry strangers, back in the days when Mobile was just a frontier outpost full of lonely Frenchmen. Teachers in Houmahatchee go on and on about them, and apparently have since Graddoch was a kid. The Cassette Girls never get mentioned in the history books after the first few chapters—they don't fight in the Creek War or get elected or anything—and generations of Alabama kids have wondered why they need to learn about this.

"I think they just want girls to have some characters to identify with in the early history," Graddoch said, flipping through my history book one morning. "I mean, you can be Julia Tutwiler. You can get sold in a slave auction, or you can get massacred at Fort Mims. The Cassette Girls are the only women in here with a happy ending."

"What's sad about Julia Tutwiler?" I said. "She made the state stop putting women and kids in men's prisons. She set up a college. She wrote the state song."

"Really?" Graddoch said. "Sing it."

"Well, I mean, I can't remember it," I said. "I heard it once."

"Wasn't super catchy, was it?" Graddoch said. "There are a million songs about Alabama and that's the worst one. None of her ideas caught on, really. We're not passionate about education or about decent prisons or any of that. Nobody wanted what she was selling."

Graddoch likes to pick on me. It's his way of making friends. He's seen my name in court documents and he knows Tutwiler is my middle name. I'm not related to Julia

Tutwiler, but I guess my parents did want what she was selling.

"And who says the Cassette Girls were happy?" I said. "Happy marrying a bunch of strangers who ordered them by mail or whatever."

"Oh, I'm sure they were happy eventually," Graddoch said. "People, if they're free, find a way to be happy eventually, even if it's not the way they originally planned."

"I guess arranged marriage is an acquired taste," I said.

"All marriage is an acquired taste," Graddoch said.

I'm getting to like Graddoch. Even when he's working, even when he's talking to a kid, he's kind of wry and warm and mean as if he was sipping bourbon in some smoke-filled room with a bunch of rich, crooked old men.

He's always saying things like: "I wouldn't trust any man who doesn't recognize and embrace the evil in his own heart. But a gentleman always trusts all women." Don't ask him why men and women are different. A gentleman doesn't explain.

"This is just sad, sad, sad, sad," Reagan said at lunch one day. "I am truly the only outlaw in this whole town. I'm your only friend who isn't, like, sixty years old."

"Graddoch's not my friend, exactly," I said. "It's not like we're painting each other's nails or something. We're working. Work friends."

"All your friends are a lot older than you," Reagan said.

"You're not older than me," I said. "Not by much, anyway."

Just then a beautiful girl from the senior class butted in.

"Hey, Reagan!" Senior Girl said. "Love your hair."

Reagan looked a little sheepish. This had become a thing. The more she did to rebel against all the cheerleader standards of beauty, the more cheerleader types seemed to like her.

For a long time, Reagan had wanted to shave most of one side of her head and flop the remaining hair over the other side—long, straight, and deep black. The school code wouldn't allow girls to shave their heads, so she found a workaround. Basically, she wore it short but not shaved on one side, then used lots of gel to slick it back flat on that side. I didn't like the haircut a lot, personally, but I told her she'd hit the mark. As long as she comes across as a girl assassin from a spy movie, she's achieved the look she wants.

Getting compliments from cheerleaders was definitely something she didn't want. And she never knew how to respond.

"Um, thanks," Reagan said to Senior Girl. "I love your very even features and uncannily perfect skin."

"That's so sweet," Senior Girl said, blinking a little like she was trying to figure out whether Reagan was serious. "Hey, are you two going to the county fair? The Future Farmers of America is selling tickets in advance as a fundraiser. Want to buy some from me?"

"It all depends," Reagan said. "Is this some kind of hokey, wholesome county fair with little kids and cotton candy and the American flag or is this a creepy county fair with weirdo carnival workers and unsafe rides where you feel like a clown is going to come out of the corn and slash you to death?"

"Umm . . . both?" Senior Girl said. "I think they're all both, aren't they? If you want to get slashed by a clown, come after dark. If you want wholesome, come before dark. If you come during the day on Saturday, you'll also get to see my little brother's pig. It's in a contest."

"Prize pigs," Reagan said. "You're tipping the scales toward hokey-wholesome there. What do they got that's creepy?"

Senior Girl winked.

"If they told you in advance, it wouldn't be creepy, would it?" Senior Girl said.

"Well played," Reagan said. "Put me down for two tickets. That way Ms. Law-and-Order here will have to come with me."

When I came home and told Taleesa I was going to the fair, she was shocked—and not at me. She simply couldn't believe all the stuff about the prize pigs.

"This can't be real," she said. "A county fair like in the movies. With like, striped tents and a pie-eating contest and Judy Garland falling in love and hay everywhere. This is some kind of scam."

"Of course it's real," Dad said. "They put up billboards for it every year. 'Strudwick County Agricultural Society Presents the County Fair.'"

Taleesa shook her head. "But I mean, really, nobody actually does all this county fair stuff for real anymore," she said. "I know that kind of sign. Yellow with the big block letters. This is just some kind of gun show all dressed up to look nice."

"Well," Dad said. "I guess every big event here seems to have gun sales involved in it somewhere."

Dad wasn't kidding. The best store in town is Guns and Fudge, which sells only—you guessed it—guns and fudge.

Really good fudge. It smells like Christmas in there, and the fudge part of the shop is always nice and chilly, and there's a big model train in the middle of the floor that runs from the fudge counter to the gun counter making little tooting sounds.

"I'm telling you, Taleesa, this is a real thing," Dad said. "There is actually a Strudwick County Agricultural Society and they actually are a bunch of old white men who farm and they really do hold a fair with rides and hay bales and contests where people judge the best fancy chicken and all that. It's real. I know it's weird. People don't have phones in their house anymore, men don't wear ties at weddings, but we've still got this, just like it looked in 1930. An unironic celebration of the soybean industry."

"How big do soybean plants get?" Martinez asked. "Big enough for a clown to hide in?"

"I don't believe you," Taleesa said. "But we're going. If you're right about this, it'll be terrific."

"Radiant," I said.

"Humble," Dad said.

▮ ▮ ▮

We don't really do autumn in Houmahatchee. At least, we don't do it all that well.

When the people on TV are starting to wear coats and see their breath in front of them in little clouds, when Charlie Brown is jumping into a pile of cartoon leaves, we're still sweating and watching the hurricane forecasts. In town, here in the historic district, there are the kinds of trees that lose their leaves in the fall. Out there in the county, it's just acres and acres of pine trees, all planted in rows and waiting for loggers to cut them down. I guess that's where you'd find an evil clown in Strudwick County, hiding among the eerie bare pine trunks. Pine trees are our corn, I guess.

But on the first night of the fair, at least, it was properly chilly. Like, fifty-five degrees or so. Cold enough that I could try on my New Look.

Okay, not my New Look, just my Look. It seemed like something I should have. For the first twelve years of my life, I just wore the same T-shirts and shorts that every other kid does. Sometimes I wore an ugly dress when I went to court. But then one afternoon, sitting in the living room with a pen and legal pad and watching old Disney sitcoms instead of working on my shelter plan, I suddenly felt this strange yearning to have a signature look of my own. Reagan had one. Teenagers on TV always had one. There were a few shows where actors who were actual twins played a pair of twins, or where one actor played both twins. You always knew which twin was which because each twin had a Look. Brainy, Macho, Fashion Plate, Hiker, Hippie. Something to make people remember you.

That got me rummaging through Taleesa's closet for hats to steal. Taleesa has tried virtually every hairstyle and fad diet known to woman, and she also owns basically every kind of clothing a freelance writer can afford. That includes a stack of hats, some of them in actual hat boxes, stuffed on a top shelf in the hallway closet. None of Taleesa's clothes fit me, but hats seemed to be fair game.

There was a big, crocheted hat for you to stuff your dreads

in, if you have dreads. There were a couple of other baggy hats that looked like something you'd wear protesting the Vietnam War, and a straight-up Army-looking green cap that Taleesa said she wore to an actual protest. In the boxes, there were beautiful church hats that were like a wedding cake for your head. For some reason, there was a bowler hat that was actually pretty neat, though it was too big for me or anybody in the family. I know because I went around the house putting it on everybody's head. Easy looked the best in it, but he wouldn't leave it on long enough for me to take his picture.

And then I found it. A rounded, blue baseball-cap sort of thing, but with a smaller brim, and with a band around it and a plum-colored felt flower on one side.

"This is the hat," I said to Taleesa. "This is me. This is my look. Girly, but girly like a girly cartoon character."

Taleesa looked skeptical.

"So, yeah," she said. "That's a women's Stormy Kromer cap. I think I should warn you: the men's version of this is in fact the hat that Elmer Fudd wears in Bugs Bunny cartoons. It is a cartoon hat."

"This is no Elmer Fudd hat," I said. "This is the Volkswagen Beetle of hats. It's got a flower that never dies. Why don't women wear these all the time?"

"It's a very warm hat," Taleesa said. "You realize, don't you, that in Milwaukee we wore hats to actually keep our heads warm? If you wear that, you'll get a band of sweat around the bottom in no time."

"My winter look, then," I said. "Whatever you do, don't tell Martinez about the Elmer Fudd thing."

With the temperature down into the fifties, the first night of the fair was my first time to try the New Look. I realized, just that afternoon, that I didn't have any girly clothes, really, to wear with my girly cap. So I put on jeans and a T-shirt and a purple windbreaker that was kind of close to the color of the flower on the hat, and I zipped it up almost to my neck. Martinez narrowed his eyes when he first saw me in the hat, but he didn't make any smart remarks. I guess I didn't look like anything he'd ever seen before so he couldn't think of a name to call me.

On the way to the fair, with the sun shining on my side of the car, it did get pretty hot. I rolled down the window a crack. With the outside now air cool and dry, instead of hot and wet like usual, you could actually smell the pine forest.

"Look at that," I said. "I really could imagine an evil clown chasing somebody through all those rows of trees. It's eerie how, when you plant a bunch of pines all close together, they'll have green stuff only at the very top. I wonder why it's like that."

"Epicormic branching," Dad said, from the driver's seat. "When the sunlight hits—"

"Stop stop stop," Martinez said. "I don't want to know why. I am sick of living in a house full of smart people. When y'all go on explaining stuff the way y'all always do, I feel like someone's drilling a hole in my head. Can't we just let trees be trees?"

"They don't stop being trees just because science understands them," I said.

"Yes," Martinez said. "Yes, they do. A killer clown can't be in a forest with unicornic branching or whatever. You're killing the fun, saying all this science stuff like 'pinus palustris.' Have some imagination."

Don't let Martinez fool you. He's one of the smart ones, too. *Pinus palustris* is the scientific name for longleaf pine. Though honestly, I think what we were looking at was probably scrub pine.

"Wait," I said. "You actually *want* a killer clown to be hiding in the forest?"

"Yes," my little brother said adamantly. "Yes, I do. Because it's fall. Because it's Halloween. We are about to go to a county fair. A circus-type thing. It's supposed to be all magic and spookiness. Can't we stop being so smart for a minute and just have some magic?"

"Taleesa," Dad said. "Your son wants to live in the demon-haunted world."

"You're the one who brought us to Alabama," Taleesa replied. I'm not entirely sure what this exchange meant, but it sounded like they were ribbing each other, not really arguing.

"I don't care what y'all do," Martinez said. "I'm going to believe everything they tell me at this fair. If they have, like, the world's strongest man or whatever, I'm going to believe it's really the world's strongest man. Because I want to actually have *fun*."

I wanted to say that people could be smart and have fun. But I couldn't, really, because I was starting to think that he was right. I mean, I'm smart enough to know that there's not really a killer clown in the woods. What would he eat? And don't say he eats kids, because he'd have to eat a kid a week or so, and surely we'd notice. And I'm not scared that the government is creating clones to control us because that's not how cloning works. I'm scared of real things, like men with guns, which you see every time you go to Walmart. I'm scared of snakes sunning themselves on the road, which I come across at least once every summer. But I'm not scared of a killer clown. I'm not scared that the Devil himself is going to appear in the headlights at night, the way so many people around here are, because I just don't think there's a Devil.

Still, I'm starting to realize that if I were a frightened girl who believed that a marionette could come alive and kill me, and if I were dumb enough to go watch a movie about that, then if I reached out my hand in the dark there'd be a boy to take it. And if I were a dumb boy who believed in this stuff, I'd be there to take a frightened girl's hand and pretend to be brave and put my arm around her and protect her even though I'm scared to death of this completely harmless thing on a movie screen. And at the end of the movie we'd be totally safe, just like we were totally safe all along, but each of us would have held a hand and pressed together and smelled another person's smell and huddled together for protection. I'm starting to understand that smart, brave people don't do this as often as they'd like.

"Okay, Martinez," I said. "I'm with you. Just this once, I'm going to just let myself go and be superstitious and scared. The demon-haunted world. Magic. It might be fun."

"What if they had a haunted house," Martinez said with some excitement, "and they had a guy who chases you with a chainsaw the way they do, and the chainsaw was supposed to not have an actual chain on it and they *forgot to take the chain off* and it was a real killer haunted house? What if they forgot to put a bolt on one of the spinny rides and one of the cars just goes sailing out into the air and the people on it get mangled and die?"

"I guess we'll just have to be brave," I said.

"I'm going to be brave," Martinez said. "I'm going to ride everything. I'm going to punch the chainsaw guy in the face."

The fairground smelled like hay. Dad had to pay a guy five bucks to park in a field between two giant pickup trucks that made our Hyundai look like a clown car. It wasn't completely dark yet, but it was dark enough that the lights of the fair in the distance looked fierce. We could see spinning rides and strings of white lights around some of the funnel cake and shoot-the-plastic-duck booths. There was a jumble of music: deep-bass booms and church organ sounds from the haunted house, and somewhere else silly calliope music, and over that, some high-pitched hair metal from the 1980s.

"Ratt," Dad said. He had a strange, dreamy smile on his face. "'Round and Round.' Wow, I haven't heard that song in years."

"I think you're alone in your emotions about this band," Taleesa joked.

Once we were out of the car, Martinez and I quickly moved out ahead of Dad and Taleesa, marching though the rutted field and passing a young couple struggling to push a stroller through this mess. My brother and I both wanted to get away from each other and our parents, so we could explore. Dad and Taleesa didn't stop us, I think, because they knew we'd come back to them for money to buy tickets to get on rides.

At the ticket booth, I saw a familiar lopsided hairdo. Reagan was there, with her dad Brad Royall, who was holding hands with a beautiful, tanned white lady with a frilly blouse and big hooped earrings. Reagan's dad was on a date—and he was wearing cargo pants and a polo shirt and an empty holster on his belt.

"Hey," Reagan said. "You look hot."

I think I blushed a little. High praise, coming from Reagan.

"Thanks," I said. "I think this hat is going to be my look from now on."

Turns out she didn't mean that kind of hot.

"It's like sixty-five degrees," Reagan said. "That hat. Isn't it something people wear when it's snowing? Like in a Christmas show on the Hallmark Channel?"

The lady with the hoop earrings turned to shake hands. Her arms literally jangled because she had three bracelets on each wrist.

"You must be Atticus," she said. "I'm Janna. It's so good to get to meet Reagan's friends."

We made small talk, got tickets, heard some lectures from the parents about sinister-clown safety and somehow, Reagan and I managed to peel away from everybody. We even managed to get away without having to take my little brother along.

"So . . . that was uncomfortable," I said. "With Janna, I mean. She kept waiting for somebody to introduce her—as girlfriend or friend or date or whatever—and neither of you said anything."

"Not my job," Reagan said curtly.

"So I take it you don't like her," I said.

"She's fine," Reagan said. "She's good-looking and she's sweet. She's age-appropriate for Dad, not some college student or whatever, so that's good. She makes Dad happy, and Dad happy makes me happy. She's not too annoying, but I can tell she wants to help me deal with grief over my mother or whatever. She told Dad that the way I dress is a cry for help."

"Ew," I said. "Grownups. Everything you do is a cry for help, and then when you actually cry or ask for help they're like, 'What got into you?'"

"If I really wanted to cry for help, I'd wear a ridiculous hat," Reagan said. "You're going to be sweating before the night is over."

"They don't sweat on the Hallmark Christmas movies," I said. "And you know they film those in the summer in California or somewhere. The snow is all fake. And looking like a Hallmark lady would be a step up for me, right. They're sexy, aren't they?"

"I guess," Reagan said. "I can't really follow those movies, because I can't tell the actors apart. They all look like Fortnite characters."

"Anyway, since when do you watch the Hallmark Channel?" I said.

"Janna," Reagan said, pointing back at her dad and his girlfriend. "Hallmark is her thing. I mean, it's okay, I don't mind having her around. But she's different. I never thought I'd miss my dad watching shows about guns and supercars. I really need a dose of freakiness and morbidity."

"You've come to the right place," I said.

There were rows and rows of booths selling Confederate

flags, T-shirts with wolves on them, fried turkey legs, knives of the sort you see on old Army patches, old Army patches with pictures of knives on them, skulls of various animals, umbrellas with swords hidden in the handle, black velvet paintings of Captain Kirk kissing Uhura, Elvis glasses with sideburns attached and Mike the Mouse chocolate-covered ice cream bars. I bought an ice cream bar out of pity, because Mike the Mouse, as drawn on the sign, seemed kind of deformed and sad, but he was as chocolately between his ears as anything from Disney.

To scare and entertain you there was the House of Actual Torture, which was really more like an RV of Actual Torture, lit inside with a red light, with recorded sounds of screams coming out of it. There was Space Kidnappers, a spinny, whirly ride of the sort that could have thrown and mangled Martinez the way he wanted. It's hard to see what that ride had to do with outer space, but the spinny cars were painted dark sparkly purple and it was covered in green lights, and I guess everyone knows that purple-and-green means aliens. There was Fall to Your Death, a loud contraption that took sixteen people strapped into NASCAR-type seatbelts and raised them up about twenty feet off the ground and let them hang upside down, screaming, for a long time. And there was Cup Noodles, a drunken-teacups thing where you sit in a giant ramen bowl and spin around to get dizzy. And there was a trailer with fluorescent stars on it marked See the World's Smallest Woman.

"That seems really tacky," I said. "I mean, lots of people are small. And some people are really small. It doesn't seem right to make a freak show out of them."

"Stop being so moral," Reagan said. "This is a carnival. This is a make-believe world where you can commit make-believe sins. Lots of people are sexy, but if it said World's Sexiest Woman, you'd go, wouldn't you, just to see what people think the world's sexiest woman would look like."

I nodded my head. I would go to see the World's Sexiest Woman. I wished they had World's Sexiest Woman instead of this other thing, which was embarrassing.

"We're going to go see this," Reagan said.

"I don't feel comfortable supporting this," I said. "I don't want to be seen in line here. I don't want to give them my money."

"For the love of Pete," Reagan said. "That's why they make you buy tickets. They've already got your money, there's no point boycotting. It's a pirate utopia with its own currency, so all your choices can be morality-free. Look, I'm paying for you anyway. Two for World's Smallest Woman."

There was no line, but I guess someone was already in there, because we had to wait a while at the door. A breeze blew while we waited, and it seemed to carry the smell of every forbidden thing on earth. Fried food and cigarettes. A sickly body odor like the neglected dogs have when they're brought into the shelter for their first bath. And a smell that I think might be beer or liquor.

"So," I said. "What do you think the Sexiest Woman on Earth would look like?"

"Me," Reagan said, without a moment's hesitation. "What do you think the World's Sexiest Woman looks like?"

My gut reaction was to say "you," but I knew that would just dig me deeper into the sidekick hole.

"Wonder Woman," I said.

Reagan nodded as if to say, "good answer." The door of World's Smallest Woman opened and two middle-aged ladies came out, giggling. We went in.

I'm not sure what I saw, exactly at least at first. We were in what looked like a dark hallway, and at the end of the hallway was some kind of weird dim window—or mirror. In the mirror, I could see a woman sitting on an overstuffed green couch calmly working on her knitting. She was pretty clearly a little person. I mean, her arms and legs seemed shorter than most people's. She and her knitting needles both seemed incredibly tiny compared to the giant couch she was sitting on.

"Hello there," she said.

"Oh, you can hear us?" I said. "Way over there?"

"Sure," the World's Smallest Woman said. "I can answer any questions you have, if you've got questions. I like your hat, by the way."

"Thanks," I said. "What's your name?"

"Okay," she said. "I can answer *almost* any question you have. But it's show business, so there's some stuff I won't tell you."

"Are you okay with this?" I asked. "I mean, does it bother you to be in a . . . I don't know."

"Freak show?" she asked. "Honey, it's work. I mean, it's a job. They pay me to talk to people. And people are pretty respectful. The funny thing is that out there, in the world, people point and whisper and I don't get paid a dime. Don't you have any questions? Like where I sleep or how I go to the bathroom or whatever?"

"Ew, no," I said. "Reagan?"

Reagan was just sitting there silent. Stunned? I don't know.

"Look," I said. "Why can't we look at you directly? What's all this mirror stuff about?"

"It's show business, kid," she said. "Just relax and go with it. There's magic in the world if you stop looking for all the mirrors. You've already paid your money, so just believe. I can tell your fortune if you want, ladies. I'm also the World's Smallest Fortune Teller."

"Yeah," Reagan said. "We want our fortunes."

"You'll have your first kiss tonight," the World's Smallest Woman said.

"Me? Her? Which one of us?" Reagan asked.

She looked up from her knitting for the first time and smiled. "Looks like your time's up," she said. "Please let the next group in."

One good thing about a hat: you can pull it down over your face and hide as you come out of some place where you don't want to be seen.

"What next?" Reagan said.

We wasted another two tickets on a booth called Elizabeth Tavoris the Amazing Movie Star Lookalike. We spent five minutes talking to a pretty white lady with short, jet-black hair who greeted us in a jockey outfit, then went behind a little barrier and did a quick change into a cool-looking Cleopatra costume and finally wound up in a gray wig and furs and a feather boa. The whole time she talked about how we'd remember her from all her famous roles and her many husbands. Reagan and I giggled the whole time.

We didn't have the heart to tell her we had no idea who she was imitating.

"The fair is truly weird," I said. "It's like a tour of a nasty old man's mind."

"I can't tell who's supposed to be a beautiful person and who's supposed to be a freak," Reagan said.

"Maybe that's the lesson," I said. "Beautiful people are freaks."

"I'm done with these shows," Reagan said. "I'm doing Fall to Your Death."

"Oooh," I said. "I don't know about that one. You know I get sick really easy. And the line is super long."

Reagan rolled her eyes. "I knew it," she said. "Ms. Moral Courage, not afraid to stand in front of a judge or get shot at, but she won't ride the teacups. This is how it's going to be. I'm going to have to do all my cliff-diving alone."

"I can't help it," I said. I was queasy about the rides already. It's a problem I have, and it's bigger than just the fair. I see kids eating chicken in the lunchroom—obvious parts of an animal—and I can't help but think about what it was like to live and die as a chicken. When I saw Gary Dudley, the man who shot at me, being escorted away in his orange uniform, I couldn't help but imagine how tough it would be to ride in a van all the way to Atmore knowing that you're going to be put in an overcrowded prison and stay there for the rest of your life and have no hope and no one to blame but yourself. I knew he deserved it, and still it made me feel sick. Watching other people do scary things makes me anxious—maybe more anxious than it makes the people doing the scary things.

"I'm going in," Reagan said. "Wait for me."

"It's a long line," I said.

"Go spend some tickets then," Reagan said, not looking back.

I looked around for a moment and took the place in. The smell of hay and fried food. Booths with stuffed animals hanging in them, all of whom seemed underinflated and sad. At the end of the row, a small circus tent, with some sort of show inside. I took a few steps toward the tent, then thought maybe I should go play a game for a stuffed animal, so I turned back. And then I changed my mind again, and turned back again. Maybe I really am a sidekick. Reagan always knows what she wants.

"You're dropping your tickets," said a voice behind me.

I looked down and saw five of Reagan's tickets on the ground. I picked them up, and then I saw him.

He couldn't have been more than fourteen, but he seemed so grown-up and confident. Only later did I realize that it was because he had his hands casually in his pockets. He was literally the only person here who wasn't loaded down with tickets and stuffed animals. I could see only his thumbs but I could tell his hands were thick and rough. His jeans were dirty here and there. He wore ugly tan work boots and a red flannel shirt and a T-shirt with a stain on the front. The T-shirt was loose at the neck, as if he'd pulled it over his head a thousand times. His head seemed big, but it was because of his really thick, blonde hair that he didn't seem to have combed at all, giving him a sort of mad-professor look. He was short for a guy, not much taller than me, with blunt features that made you sort of imagine him in a mugshot.

I couldn't decide whether he was beautiful or ugly, but somehow I was in love right then and there.

"I like your hat," he said.

"It's hot," I said. "I mean, like, too hot to wear a warm hat."

He shrugged. Yes, stubby rough hands. One of them reached for his red shirt.

"It's too hot for this, too," he said. "I guess we both have a thing for flannel. I'm Emory, by the way."

Emory, two syllables. His accent reminded me of old people, when they look at Reagan's cross-stitch and call it "imbraudry," instead of embroidery. Thick as Dad's accent when he's mad.

"Where are you from?" I blurted out. "I mean, I'm sorry, I don't think I've ever seen you at school."

"I'm homeschooled," he said. "Or maybe kind of homeless-schooled. It's complicated. Where are you from?"

I laughed. "Well, I mean, I'm from Houmahatchee," I said. "Wait, so you don't know me?" I realized immediately how pompous that sounded. But I was used to strangers coming up and telling me they'd seen me in the newspaper or online. Like my mother before me, I am a prominent local weirdo.

"How can I know you?" he said. "You haven't told me your name."

"Atty," I said.

"Atty," he said, rubbing his hand on his chin sarcastically. "Should I have heard of you? Do you have some kind of . . . reputation?"

"Well, that's kind of rude," I said. "And sexist, and . . . oh, wait. Wait. You're FLIRTING with me, aren't you? Is this flirting? Is this what flirting is?"

The wry look disappeared from his face and for a moment he seemed nervous. Then it was like a light came on in his head.

"Yes," he said, nodding his head vigorously. "Yes, to be perfectly clear and honest, I am flirting with you. Do you wish to continue?"

"I'm sorry, I've never flirted before," I said. "Whether I wish to continue is for me to know and you to find out. And whether I have a reputation is also for me to know and for you to find out."

"Very good," he said. "A little mystery. Are you sure this is your first time flirting?"

"That's for me to know and . . . oh, wait, I can't do that a third time, can I," I said.

"You can do whatever you want," he said.

I can't tell you where it went from there. More wordplay. We walked up and down the rows of attractions, swapping flirty words like that, and I never really learned anything about him or told him anything about me, but I felt connected in a way I never felt connected to a boy before. He was smart and confident. I kept thinking he'd make a good lawyer.

We passed Reagan's dad and Janna the Girlfriend, and they didn't even notice us. They were walking along just staring and smiling at each other. She was carrying a giant pink stuffed bear that he'd no doubt won for her. It was so big she kind of waddled as she walked.

Emory noticed me looking at them.

"They're on a date," he said, matter-of-factly. "When they win a prize on a date, she's always the one that carries it. When a married couple wins a bear, she always makes him carry it."

"Really?" I said, still trying to sound flirty and teasy. "You seem so sure about that. Do you, like, come to the fair a lot?"

"Look, let me win you one of them bears," he said. He grabbed my hand—thrill!—and led me toward a booth. "How about this shooting game? I'm good at shooting."

I just nodded. The hand-holding caught me off guard. It was like warm fluid rushed from my hand to my brain with the speed of an electric shock, and then the warmth started flowing down the rest of my body. I didn't really want to think much right then. Just nod.

I guess I blanked out a bit because everything seemed to go so fast. Emory talked to the guy who operated the shooting gallery. I don't remember Emory paying any tickets. He plinked at the passing ducks and hit probably about half of them. And the carnival guy reached up and grabbed a big powder-blue bear out of the top row above the shooting gallery. I know you have to hit targets all night to win one of those things, but it seemed like he won it fast, in just one game. Before I knew it, he was holding this giant thing out in front of me. I guess he noticed how stunned I looked.

"Yes, it's for you," he said. "I won you a bear. Take it. Or do you want me to carry it?"

Something very strange was happening. Is it possible to be pleasantly embarrassed? I was turning red and I was happy. I couldn't help but think about what he'd said earlier about who, in the couple, carries the bear.

"Yes," I said. "I very much want you to carry my bear. I

mean, not in that way. I mean, maybe in that way, but not for a long time. I mean . . . look, I'll take the bear. Thank you."

Something even stranger was happening now. I was leaning forward, toward him. I was going to kiss him, without even asking if I could or should. But I'm clumsy, and I just sort of bumped him with the bear.

"Pillow fight!" said a voice behind me. It was Martinez, standing at a funnel cake booth across the aisle. Taleesa was with him. She looked at me with a little interest and a little worry, but she shuffled my little brother away.

"I know we don't look alike," I said. "But that's my little brother. And my stepmom."

Emory laughed a nervous laugh.

"It sort of reminds me," Emory said. "I hate to do this, but I have something I've got to do with my family. I'm actually kind of late." He felt around in his pockets and pulled out a slip of paper and a pen. He put the paper on the bear and began to write.

"Here's my number," he said. "If you ever need someone to carry your bear, call me."

"Wait, let me give you mine," I said.

"I'm actually seriously late to meet my family," he said, beginning to step away. "Text your number to me."

"What if I lose this?" I asked. This slip of paper, a number on an old receipt, was suddenly very important to me.

"I really do come to the fair a lot," he said. "Maybe I'll be here."

And then he was gone. It was just me and my bear. This flimsy, too-shiny overstuffed bear that I loved so much just then, more than I've ever loved any living animal.

■ ■ ■

I waddled away, in the direction where I last saw Taleesa and Martinez. It was literally hard to walk with the bear, which was light but hard to get a grip on.

"Next time I fall in love, I'm getting a bear with handles," I muttered to myself.

I caught up with Taleesa and Martinez in front of a drink stand. Now Dad and Reagan were with them too.

"No, Martinez, you can't sue the fair," Dad said.

"But it's called Fall to Your Death, and nobody died," Martinez said. "It's fraud. I should at least get my tickets back."

"I'm with the kid on this one," Reagan said. "It wasn't even remotely scary. Hey, what's this *giant bear?*"

Martinez shrugged. "Some boy won Atty a bear," he said.

"Well, that's kind of a sexist assumption," Dad said. "Your sister's plenty capable of winning a bear all by herself."

"But I saw them—" Martinez started, before Taleesa shoved a fistful of tickets in front of him. She looked at me with a strange, knowing smile that I've mostly seen her give only to other grownups.

We don't hide things in my family, generally, and my dad isn't the kind of guy who's going to go off in a jealous rage when his daughter starts dating. He's not a gun-polisher. But frankly I don't think any of us want to know what he *will* do in certain situations. He'll find a way to make it weird somehow. We all know that *he* doesn't want to know.

As we strolled on, Reagan mouthed at me: "A boy won you a bear?" I could tell she was surprised and delighted, even before I nodded. Then she mouthed something else I couldn't make out. Finally, she had to lean in and whisper: "Did you kiss him?"

"Nope," I said in a normal voice. "Our fortune-teller was wrong."

"Maybe," Reagan said. "Or maybe that means one of us still has it coming."

We strolled through the Strudwick County Agricultural Showplace, an aluminum-sided warehouse at the middle of the fairground. There was straw on the floor, fancy chickens in little cages, soft white piglets running around in circular pens and the most beautiful, clean cows you ever saw, led around in a corral by teenagers in 4-H vests. As a vegetarian, I'm not a fan of the farm animal thing, but these show animals seemed about as well-cared-for as I've seen a pig or cow being cared for.

"Imagine if a farm was just a place for pigs to live," I said. "Imagine how happy that world would be."

"Happy but stinky," Reagan said. "It smells like manure in here."

I didn't notice the smell. Too much time in the animal shelter, I guess. I suppose I did scrunch my nose up a little at the chickens. You know you spend a lot of time with animals when you prefer some types of poop smells to others.

Coming out of the other side of the Showplace, we saw a bigger corral outside, with a long line of people in front of it, tickets in hand. At the end of that line was a scaffold of sorts, and a pudgy white guy in shorts and a stained Oxford shirt and a safari hat stood atop the scaffold, taking tickets. A sign out front read: "ELIZABETH III, QUEEN OF THE ELEPHANTS."

And then she came into view. An elephant, being led slowly in a circle around the corral. She was smaller than I thought a full-grown elephant would be. I guess my mental image of an elephant is a big bull elephant like on the University of Alabama football gear, with big ears flared out. This elephant had a different kind of ears, sort of like wings of a giant bat folded to the side. On her back, there was a padded saddle with bars, where a mom and two kids sat. Pay your ticket, ride the elephant.

"I'm guessing you're not into riding elephants," Reagan said.

I didn't say anything. Something had taken hold of me. I walked ahead of everyone else, toward the corral. I got there just as Elizabeth walked past, her walk smooth and graceful but also sad. One big brown eye swiveled around to look at me, and kind of went right past me, as if I were just another self-absorbed carnival chick holding a bear while Elizabeth worked.

"She's suffering," I said, before anyone else caught up with me. Then, to Dad. "Dad, this elephant doesn't want to be here."

Dad sighed.

"I'm not a fan of this," he said. "I'm definitely not going to participate. But I don't know that she's suffering. I mean, how do you know they're not taking care of her behind the scenes?"

"I just know," I said. "Go back in there and look those little piggies in the eye. And then come out here and look at Elizabeth. There's a difference."

Just then, Taleesa and Martinez caught up. "Oh," Taleesa said. "Oh, man, that elephant looks sad."

Martinez: "I want to ride the sad elephant."

"No," Dad and Taleesa said in unison.

We watched in silence as Elizabeth swished for another full turn around the corral.

"That *is* a sad elephant," Martinez said. "No, I don't want to ride that."

"You know how I said I was going to believe in scary clowns and magic tonight?" I said.

"Yeah," Martinez said.

"Well, what if I told you this elephant is talking to me? She's telling me she wants to be free," I said. "Miss Megg is always saying we should be careful about assuming that we know what animals want. But this is different. She's communicating with me."

The big eye swept past me again as Elizabeth walked past. It said to me: *if you are who you say you are, help me.*

"I've got to free this elephant," I said.

CHAPTER THREE

◇

Reagan came home with us after a quick stop at her house to pick up a toothbrush and medicine and pajamas. The sleepover wasn't something Reagan and I planned. Apparently Janna and Reagan's dad quietly came to Dad and Taleesa and suggested it so they could spend some time alone.

"I don't understand Christianity," I said, as we waited in the car for Reagan to collect her things. "I mean, church people are always talking about waiting until marriage and all that, but when grownups want to spend the night together, they just go ahead and do it."

Dad shrugged.

"I'm not inclined to judge," he said. "They're not hurting anybody really. Let 'em have a little happiness. What is it Reagan says? I am large, I contain multitudes?"

"I want to join a religion where nobody talks about this icky stuff at all," Martinez said.

Reagan returned to the car, pill bottle in hand, arms wrapped around a little purple girly duffel bag stuffed with clothes and toiletries. She plopped down in the seat next to me, looking completely unlike Reagan. She was sad, vulnerable, a little girl.

"Well, this is awkward," she growled.

"Atty, give your bear to Martinez," Dad said. "Now that you're sitting in the middle, you're blocking the rear view."

"Ugh," said Martinez. "I don't want your yucky love bear."

"Everybody knows what's happening here, don't they?" Reagan said. "How is this happening? I'm the hottest person around, and I'm the only person who's not getting any action tonight."

Dad turned to look through the back window as he backed out of the Royalls' driveway.

"I think you're exaggerating, Reagan," he said. "I don't think *everybody's* having romance tonight."

Taleesa looked back at me, cautiously, clearly ready to change the subject.

"That elephant," she said. "How can they do that? Isn't there a law or something?"

"I've been thinking about that," I said. "I've read all of Title 3 of the Code of Alabama, and I can't recall a thing about elephants in it."

"Well," Dad said. "As we know, Title 3 isn't the only part about animals. There's the Fish and Game Section as well. And there's the Administrative Code."

All of Alabama law is in a set of books called the Code of Alabama 1975, which—on our bookshelves at least—takes up about six feet of shelf space. Well, six feet with a gap of about three inches, because I always carry "Title 3—Animals" with me. There's a whole other set of books, called the Administrative Code, that explains the stuff in the Code to mayors and cops and other people who actually have to do all the work. All of this is online, and I've gotten pretty good at looking things up on my phone.

"Here it is," I said. "Section 220-2-26. Let's see . . . any species of mongoose, San Juan rabbits, it shall be unlawful to release any tame turkey, walking catfish . . . no, that's not it. Here it is: 'permits for wildlife for public exhibition.' Is an elephant an ungulate? Oh, yes it is, it's listed here. There it is: you have to have a permit to exhibit an ungulate, which includes rhinos, hippos, elephants and something called a cape buffalo."

"Super Cow," Martinez said. "A buffalo with a cape."

"If there's a permit required to display an elephant, then there's probably some sort of inspection that has to take place," Dad said. "Somebody from the state ought to be able to inspect the elephant's living conditions and approve or disapprove."

"No wait," I said. "There's a list of who's exempt from getting a permit. Zoos or wildlife exhibits, private traveling zoos, circuses, pet shops. Jeez, basically anybody who would own an elephant is exempt from the elephant permit."

"Well," Taleesa said, "there's got to be something we can do. First thing in the morning, let's get into the books again."

▮ ▮ ▮

At first, Reagan was a little crabby as we settled in to sleep. She's always like that on sleepovers. And now there's the problem of Easy. He won't let anyone on the bed but me, so that messes up our old arrangement of me on the floor, Reagan in the bed. If I'm in the bed and Reagan's on the floor, he sits there and glares at Reagan like she's going to attack me. So in the end, both of us were on the floor with Easy between us.

"What's it like to have a stepmom?" Reagan asked.

"I don't know," I said. "I mean, really. I always talk about Taleesa as a stepmom because of the color thing. It's the quickest way to make people understand. But she's my MOM, for real. I've never known anything but having them around, Taleesa and Martinez. I remember being mad when they told me I was a big girl and Martinez gets to ride in the shopping cart instead of me. But I don't remember ever riding in the shopping cart myself. My other mom is, I don't know, a ghost. A lady that I was cloned off of, who left notes in the margins of all of our books. It's just not the same."

Reagan was quiet.

"There's a lot about my mom that I guess I don't remember," she said. "Stuff that I don't remember clearly, anyway. It's weird. All the times when things were really bad, all my memories of those times, I'm not seeing them from inside my own head. They're all like movies. Like I'm watching them from outside of me."

"Toni, my therapist, keeps asking me about this," I said. "Dissociation. That's when you see yourself from outside like that. It's supposed to be a thing that happens when you have post-traumatic stress disorder."

Reagan was quiet again for a moment.

"Is this good or bad?" she said. "I mean, I think I kind of

like it. I like thinking of myself from the outside. I'd really rather be Outside Reagan right now, looking at this cool kid who's giving everybody a hard time, instead of being Inside Reagan, moping around and thinking about what it's like to have a stepmom."

"So that's how all this works?" I said. "Tough Reagan. Smart-alecky Reagan. Reagan who will always take a dare or eat a bug or whatever. It's all just to avoid dealing with what's inside."

"Don't knock it," Reagan said. Her voice was starting to get that edge again, sounding like she normally sounds instead of like a hurt little kid. "Maybe there's nothing inside. Nothing worth dealing with. Ever talk to Toni about that? What if inside is just a bunch of broken furniture and it will never be fixed and there's no point in trying?"

"I don't know," I said. "Today I feel like there *is* something inside. Something warm and comfy."

Reagan poked me in the side with a finger. Easy snapped at her, with one click of the jaws.

"Warm and comfy because you're in luuuv," she said. "You got you a maaaan. Gettin' some action."

I smiled in the dark, but I turned away a little.

"Maybe I've got me a man," I said. "I don't think I want to talk about it just yet. I don't want to talk it all away."

"I've really got to know about this boy who wants to win a bear for a girl who wears an Elmer Fudd hat," Reagan said. "What's he like? What's his name?"

"Emory," I said

"Emory what?" Reagan said.

"We didn't get that far," I said.

"But he won you a whole bear," Reagan said. "That takes a long time. And you didn't get his whole name."

"It didn't take that long," I said. "He's skillful. He has rough hands, like someone who works. He's rough, like the fair, in a good way. He smelled like hay."

"So he doesn't mind a girl who smells like dogs all the time," Reagan said.

"Do I smell like dogs?" I asked. Of course I did. I was sleeping with a dog right next to me. I have dog hair all over everything I own.

"But you didn't kiss him, even though the world's smallest lady said you would," Reagan said. "Did he try to kiss you?"

" Yes, and the bear kind of got in the way," I said. "Look, I don't think I want to talk about it. It was nice. I want to keep it for myself. Anyway, what about you? Did you hunt yourself up a man, Miss Outside-My-Own-Body?"

"You're afraid," Reagan said, poking me again. "You're afraid of magic. You don't want the World's Smallest Woman to be right."

"I'm not afraid of magic," I said. "Right now, just now, I really like magic. Maybe I am afraid of other things. I mean, like, I've never thought about it until now, but there are people who are good at kissing and people who are bad at kissing, right? What if it turns out I'm not good at it?"

Reagan was quiet again.

"This is where you're supposed to tell me not to worry about it," I said. "This is where you're supposed to tell me that guys don't care whether you're good or not."

"Well," Reagan said. "I'm not gonna do that. Maybe it does matter. Maybe there's a skill and we're both bad at it and we'll be lonely freaks our whole lives because we're not good at it. I'll live alone in a big gothic house, and men will pine over me, and they'll never know my dark secret, which is that I never learned how to kiss."

I chuckled. "Well, I mean, how are you supposed to learn anyway?" I said. "I see things in books about people practicing on pillows and stuff. That seems stupid."

"I don't know," Reagan said. "You would have to practice with somebody, and you can't because if you do then it's not practice anymore. I always figured those girly-girl types—Peyton Vebelstadt and her friends—practiced on each other or something."

She meant to make me giggle, but something else happened to me. Thinking of Emory, the almost-kiss, and Peyton Vebelstadt all together in one strange moment, I suddenly couldn't catch my breath. In a good way. I let out a big, deep, pleasant sigh.

"I would kiss Peyton Vebelstadt," I said. I couldn't believe I said that, but it was true.

Reagan was quiet again, for a long time. I lay there with my back turned to Reagan, feeling a thousand emotions at once. I realized, all of a sudden, that I really was in love with Emory. True love, like in the movies. The once-in-a-lifetime kind, the kind you can't mess up. Only I realized it just as I had cheated on him—cheated by imagining myself kissing someone else. I wanted to rush out the door and run down the road to the fair and find Emory and—and what then? Apologize? Kiss him? I didn't know. I just felt wild. And I was expecting Reagan to give me heck, to tease me mercilessly about cheating on the boy I hadn't even kissed.

I waited and listened. And finally I realized she was asleep. The little snore I was hearing, it wasn't Easy. It was Reagan, dozing off.

▮ ▮ ▮

The next morning, everyone woke to the sound of me screaming.

"WHERE IS IT?" I shouted to Reagan, who was still sleeping. I grabbed the big stuffed bear and shook him. "WHERE DID I PUT IT?"

Here's what happened. When I woke up, I had one thing on my mind: send a text to Emory. That's what he'd told me to do. He gave me his number, and asked me to text my number to him.

So I hopped up and went over to where my pants were lying on the floor. Nothing in the pockets. Shirt pocket: nothing. I even checked the folds in my hat. Nothing there either. I checked my purse, even though I hadn't even brought my purse to the fair. And only then did I realize that being calm and checking all the normal places wasn't going to help.

My chance for a love life was on a little slip of paper. That piece of paper was somewhere between the fairground and here. My future life played out before me in an instant: I could have grown up to be a fairly normal person, with two children and a wedding ring, if only I had hung on to this little love-receipt. Instead, that slip of paper was out in the parking field behind the fairground, stuck to a piece of dried hay and flopping randomly in the wind. If I go back to get it, surely by the time I arrive the wind will pick back up and carry the paper away. Some other girl will marry Emory, and one day in fifty years he'll wonder why the girl with the funny hat never called him back, and he'll shrug.

"Let's just be calm," Taleesa said. "Here are my keys. Go look in the car. I'm making coffee."

There was no paper in the car, though Martinez was delighted to discover that I found an old Iron Man toy, in pristine condition, between the back seat cushions. He'd lost it literally the first day he bought it, two years ago.

At breakfast, I could do nothing but stare into my bowl of Froot Loops and almond milk. No one seemed as crushed by the death of my future family as I was. At least Dad had an excuse for being so casual. He still didn't know anything about Emory.

"I had a dream about the elephant," Dad said. "It was weird. In my dream, they told me Elizabeth the Elephant wasn't Elizabeth at all. He was a he, his name was Saramago and he was an eighty-nine-year-old Portuguese elephant, which they said is smaller and drier than an African or Indian elephant. That's what they said. It's a very dry and long-lived elephant."

"I don't think there is such a thing as a Portuguese elephant," Taleesa said.

"No, I don't think so either," Dad said. "But it has got me thinking. Elephants do live a long time. And they're not from Alabama. There must be quite a story behind Elizabeth. And I don't even know where to start with that. I mean, we're pretty good at researching and investigating things, all of us. But with this, where do we start?"

"Surely there's got to be some kind of elephant registry or something," Taleesa said. "Some kind of paperwork."

"We've got to go back to the fair," I said, still staring into my cereal. "Yes, that's it. We've got to go back to the fair and look into this. That's the way to pick up where we left off."

And so it was agreed. Some of us, at least, were headed back to the fair. Me, of course. Taleesa said she wanted to go, and naturally Martinez wasn't going to pass up a chance to try and Fall To His Death again. Reagan opted out, saying she wanted to get her house back from Janna.

"And of course I wouldn't want to get in the way of the love birds," Reagan said later, in my room, as she was packing up her things. "I know the real reason you want to go back to the fair."

I felt a twinge of guilt. And something else. Does it really do any good to name emotions? Sometimes there are so many of them, all at once. I sighed again.

"I'm not going to see him," I said. "He won't be there. I've lost his number. I've ruined my love life."

Reagan shrugged. "Well, there's always Peyton Vebelstadt," she said.

"Wait," I said. "What's that supposed to mean?"

"Oh, you know," Reagan said. "You're gay. You've been crushing on Peyton ever since I've known you. I really just figured it out last night, when you said that thing about her."

"I don't think I'm gay," I said. "I'm in love with Emory. He is, in fact, a boy. Oh, God. I am in love. With a boy I'll never see again."

"You're in denial," she said. "You like girls and boys. That makes you gay."

I shrugged.

"Well, I mean, yes," I said. "I like girls and boys. I don't think I'm in denial about anything, though."

"So, you're bi," Reagan said. "You're bisexual. No need to be ashamed. You need to come out. To let the world know who you are."

I shook my head. "I don't think it works that way," I said. "I don't feel any particular need to declare anything."

"That is how it works, though," she said. "First you realize you're gay, then you come out to friends, then you tell your parents and so on."

"That's *not* how it works," I said. "I don't think you understand my family. Nobody ever assumed I was straight. From the beginning, Dad and Taleesa were always like, 'when you grow up and marry some boy or some girl.' They were always cool with it. Everybody's free to love whoever they want. There's no need to make some kind of declaration."

"So if you just came home with a chick and said, hey, this is my girlfriend, your parents would be cool with it?" Reagan asked.

"Yes," I said. "Honestly, I think Dad would probably be more comfortable with that than with, you know, Emory."

"Who we still haven't really told him about," Reagan said. "See, you're even in the closet with the straight stuff."

"I don't think it's a closet," I said. "I think there are just a lot of things we don't talk about."

Reagan shook her head.

"You're in the closet," she said.

Chapter Four

◇

If I could drive a car, I would have jumped right in and raced to the fairgrounds immediately. It didn't matter that the fairground was closed, and would be until late in the afternoon. I would have spent the day walking around the parking lot, looking for that slip of paper.

I can't drive, though. I quietly asked Taleesa about the possibility of going early, but I knew what she was going to say. She's good at reining me in when my mind races. When we're leaving the house and I want to check for a second and third time to make sure the front door is locked, she's the one who threatens to leave without me.

"Don't you have work to do?" she said. "Shouldn't you be looking up stuff about elephants? We know what happens when you get started on a project without researching everything first."

She didn't specifically mention the turkey-pardoning incident, but I knew that was what she was talking about. It was not my finest hour.

Every year at Thanksgiving, the governor of Alabama

offers a "pardon" to a pair of Thanksgiving turkeys. She'll hold a meeting on the lawn of the Capitol, with Clyde and Henrietta—the turkeys are always named Clyde and Henrietta—in cages nearby. And she'll wish everyone a happy Thanksgiving and announce that she's using her power as governor to cancel the execution of these two turkeys.

I know it's supposed to be cute, but it turns my stomach. First of all, a pardon is a kind of mercy that a governor offers to somebody who'd been convicted of a crime—and we all know that Clyde and Henrietta have not committed a crime. They're just turkeys.

It's even more icky when you consider the fact that in Alabama we actually do execute human beings. The death penalty is supposed to be for people who commit murder, but there are innocent people who get convicted of murder—it almost happened to Jethro Gersham—and it's just weird to kill people in order to send a message not to kill people. The governor doesn't actually have a lot of power to pardon people of most criminal charges, but she does have the power to change a death sentence to a life sentence. Governors almost never do this. Fischer King, nice as he seemed in person, signed every execution order that came across his desk. When King left and Luxapallila Magby became governor, I hoped maybe she'd see things differently, because she seems like a nice old lady. I mean, she's a former schoolteacher, she doesn't talk all that macho talk like the men who run for office, and she's notorious for hugging everybody she meets. So far, though, no luck. Turns out you can be a hugger and still sign an order that sends a guy to his death.

In Strudwick County, we get the whole week of Thanksgiving off school, which meant I was free on the day of the turkey-pardoning. So I convinced Dad and Taleesa to rent me a turkey suit. This was not easy to do, as it turned out, because I'd ruined a pig suit just a month before. My plan was to stand outside the turkey-pardoning event holding a sign that said, simply, "SICK." I had a lot of complicated things to say, and in my experience, television stations love to give screen time to a kid dressed like a farm animal.

But I didn't do enough research. Anybody can hold a sign on the sidewalk, which was my plan, but it turns out you can also get a permit to host a big rally on the Capitol steps—and that space was already reserved. When we arrived, there were a bunch of weirdos with Confederate flags marching on Dexter Avenue, giving speeches about how Alabama should become its own country. I told these guys how dumb they were being. As a result, the only thing that wound up on TV was a shot of a kid in a turkey costume being chased down Dexter Avenue by a crowd of guys in Civil War uniforms.

Things seem to work better when I read and think first. Plan first, buy the costume later.

First, find every book in the house that you can think of that might give you more information about elephants. Every book. Dad's old Collier's Encyclopedia, Volume 5, E-Emer, a big heavy book with a musty smell and thin pages that easily cut your fingers. Taleesa's old college biology textbook. A Dumbo board book from when Martinez was a baby. Any law book that might remotely apply. Stack them all on the kitchen table. Open the laptop. Read and write. Research.

Try not to think about Emory. His hands, his face so close to mine.

I did learn a few things. First: despite Dad's dream, there is no such thing as a Portuguese elephant. Elephant in Portuguese is "elefante." There are elephants in Angola, a country in southwest Africa that, long ago, was conquered by people from Portugal, and where a lot of folks still speak Portuguese today. There was a war in Angola that lasted decades and it was a big threat to the elephants there, apparently.

The elephants in Angola are African elephants. That's the kind of elephant you see in the University of Alabama logo. Actually, there are two different kinds of elephant in Africa, a kind that lives in the forest and a kind that lives on the savanna. The only other kind of elephant is the Asian elephant, with smaller ears than the African elephant, with its tallest point at the tip of its head, not at its shoulder. The females don't have tusks. That's Elizabeth, I concluded, an Asian elephant.

Some elephants live in preserves in Africa or in forests in southern Asia, but everywhere in the world you'll find elephants living in the margins of human society, like a person with a criminal record. In the US, there's a still-living elephant named Happy, born in Thailand in 1971, who was captured as a baby and sold to another zoo and then another. She worked in Florida, giving people rides and participating in tug-of-war shows, then she moved to a zoo in the Bronx. Another elephant from the same show was put to sleep after attacking other elephants. In 2005, scientists did an experiment with Happy to see if she could recognize herself in a mirror—a sign that someone is self-aware, like you and me. She passed the test.

What does self-aware mean? That's a bit hard to explain, but when you get it, you get it. Let's say you've never seen yourself in a mirror, but then I paint a red dot on your forehead and put you in front of a mirror. If you reach out with your trunk and touch the red dot on your own head, that's a sign that you're thinking: "Oh, I'm the elephant in the mirror with the red dot." Not every animal does this. Knowing that you're an elephant is one of most human things an animal can do.

Happy's not the only well-known elephant living in this country. There's also Curio, an African elephant captured in Zimbabwe in 1981 and brought to Kansas by a millionaire who wanted to start an American herd of elephants on the Great Plains. The millionaire went broke and Curio wound up as the property of a corporation that owns campgrounds all over the Southeast. At one point, Curio broke loose from her campground and smashed through the window of a gas station in Tennessee.

There are elephants on transfer trucks right now, riding from carnival site to carnival site. Some of them are older than Dad and Taleesa. Elephants often live more than fifty years, and sometimes up into their seventies. All of them were born in faraway places like Kenya or India or Myanmar and brought here decades ago. It's likely that when Elizabeth arrived here, there were no computers in people's houses, people had tape players in their cars, and a phone was a thing on the wall of your kitchen. What sort of story does an elephant have after all those years? What is Elizabeth's story?

I tried to look up Elizabeth III the Elephant on the internet and came up with nothing. I'd need to know who owned her in order find a business license or old news stories about past carnivals.

I did find a lot of photos of the Queen of England riding elephants, something she did more of than you might expect. And I found something called the Elephant and Rider Problem, which is a theory a psychologist came up with. Basically the idea is that when we make big decisions, we really make the decision with our gut, with instinct, and then we look for logic that supports the gut decision. In other words, they're saying that the elephant is the big, brainless, emotional part and the human rider is the cool brainy part that should be in control.

"Who came up with this?" I said. "Does this psychologist know anything about actual elephants?"

Dad shrugged. "I'm guessing not," he said. "But I do think there's a thing we should consider here. Are we letting emotions drive us? Did we make a gut decision—that keeping an elephant captive is wrong—and then work our way toward some sort of logical idea that it's immoral?"

"We absolutely did," Martinez said. "Elizabeth the Elephant looked each one of us right in the eye and said 'help me.' We all heard it."

I nodded. I guess I wasn't the only one who heard it.

"But we still need to think," Dad said. "What does it mean, to help Elizabeth? How do you free an elephant?"

"You get off her damn back," Taleesa said.

"But beyond that," Dad said. "What does freedom look like? I mean, certainly we're not saying they should set an elephant loose in Alabama, in late fall. And I guess going back to India or wherever she was born probably isn't an option, if Elizabeth hasn't lived in those places since she was a baby. So what *is* the right place for her?"

I felt, for a moment, like I was struggling to keep my head above water. This happens to me sometimes. I start working on a project, like the constitutional amendment thing I'm doing with Graddoch, and it leads to a bunch of reading about the history of how things got where they are. You think you're dealing with a problem from today and then you realize you're dealing with a problem that came about because of slavery or the Creek War and then you find that those things have roots in wars that happened back in Africa or Europe. You start to feel that a hundred years ago isn't that long ago and that it may take another hundred to make things really better.

Dad seemed to sense that I was feeling nervous. He put his hand on my shoulder.

"Don't worry," he said. "When you have trouble making decisions, it's usually because you need more information. Let's keep on collecting information."

▮ ▮ ▮

When you're in love, you suddenly realize that all the songs on the radio are about love.

And you understand why. Why an uptown girl, whatever that is, would take a chance on a backstreet guy, whatever that is. Why we could make a snowman and pretend that he is Parson Brown. Why Britney Spears must confess that her Lonely Ness is killing her now. But, you know, she still believes.

"If you will be here," I whispered to myself in the back seat, my fingers crossed. "And give me a sign." Instinctively I glanced over at Martinez, expecting him to make fun of me, but he had headphones on and was playing a video game.

You only hear old, old songs on the radio. Maybe this is just a Houmahatchee thing. Dad says the radio here plays all the same songs he heard on the radio in his hometown when he was a kid. We have thirteen religious stations, a public radio station with orchestra music, and three or four classic rock and oldies stations. You know you live in a small town when the coolest music is on a station owned by the Emergency Management Agency. Between commercials about getting vaccinated and ordering a weather radio, they play Billy Joel, David Bowie, Nina Simone, and Frank Sinatra.

The word "love" is in just about every one of those old songs, and there are never any words that have to be bleeped out.

"When I was a kid," Dad always says, "it was kind of rude to sing about wanting just sex, so everything was about love. Love songs were 90 percent of music. Even people who didn't care about love sang about love."

I guess a lot of radio and TV is about love even now. If you count twerking and related activities as potentially part of love, then I think we're still in the 90 percent range. I mean, if love is the "special connection" they're looking for on The Bachelor, then a lot of reality TV is about love. And there's the Hallmark Channel, which is very clear about what it takes to get love. You have to be in a small town, you have to be fit and single with a good job, you have to be in your mid-thirties, and you have to have a nice, expensive-looking winter coat. Actually, movies generally are about those people. But you can go to Walmart in Houmahatchee and shop for an hour and you're not likely to see two people like that. You'll see twentysomethings in sweats with their kids, old people who cough a lot, trollish-looking girls like me and too-eager kids like Martinez, who are maybe the only people who are really excited to be at Walmart. But real small towns don't contain a lot of young, single, fit people with good coats.

Taleesa watches Hallmark all the time, but she never talks about love. She and Dad laugh about the goofy world of the Hallmark shows. Every woman's a bestselling author and every man's either a carpenter or a small-town sheriff. Farms are clean, neat, cozy. People get stuck in small villages for strange reasons, like because a train broke down or a snow-avalanche blocked the one highway out of town. I've never seen snow or ridden on a train, but I have a feeling those things don't happen very often. They certainly don't happen here.

Dad and Taleesa love to pick those things apart. They don't pick at the love story, though. They don't say love is unrealistic or that these relationships are impossible. Still, they're full of snarky remarks about how these couples will act in five or ten years, or about how much money they must have to live the way they do.

"This lady doesn't have problems," Taleesa will say. "Even if she doesn't get this model-looking man, she's still got a big house and a great job. There are other men."

The grownups in my life don't have a lot of encouraging things to say about love at all.

"There are seventy-eight cards in a Tarot deck, and The Lovers is only one," Miss Megg told me once, while we were working at the animal shelter.

I looked up The Lovers card—don't do it, it's embarrassing to look at!—and then I looked up some others.

"So what you're saying is that I'm as likely to become a Priestess or the Queen of Swords as I am to become a Lover," I said.

"My husband and I got married by a female chaplain, and all my bridesmaids were in full dress uniform," Megg said. "So that's one priestess, four ladies with swords, and just two lovers. You do the math."

It's pretty clear that grownups are trying very hard to scrub all evidence of romance out of kid culture. In *Frozen*, they want us to see that the real love is the love between family, and in *Princess and the Frog* we learn that love is something you need to make time for while following your real dream. But every Disney princess before that was ride-or-die about falling in love. It's all they studied, all they dreamed about.

I asked Taleesa about that on our way back to the fair.

"Well," Taleesa said. "It wasn't a good model, teaching kids that they absolutely have to be with that One Special Person. I think a lot of us never really believed that story, as kids. I mean, we live in a world where parents split up sometimes, and a judge asks you whether you want to live with your mom or dad, and I think when you're in that situation it's kind of hard to believe that happiness is a mermaid marrying a prince. And then there are other folks, who grow up in a house where both of the parents stay together.

And they watch these movies and they think they've got to find that One Special Person and they've got to find them *now*. Dating someone like that can be really weird. I mean, when someone's twenty years old and they're upset that they haven't found their future spouse yet, that's weird."

I gulped. Because all of a sudden I realized I had become one of those people. Overnight. I wanted Emory like Aladdin wanted Jasmine. I wanted him like Ariel wanted legs and love.

I don't want to live without you, sang some old pop star on the radio. I get it now, what these songs are saying. You can live without love, but you'll just be some boring chick who cleans up dog poop and writes legal briefs. All of the magic, all of the mystery, is there between two lovers and nowhere else.

"It's weird that there's no Love character in *Inside Out*," I said. "There's Joy, Sadness, Disgust, Anger and Fear. That's supposed to be all the basic emotions. But they left love out."

"Well, there's Sadness," Taleesa said. "I mean, between Sadness and Joy, there you go. You've got Love."

I sighed. "It's depressing that you mention Sadness first," I said.

"It's not so bad," she said. "I love Old Martinez. And I miss him. It's strange, but a lot of times I feel good being sad about my father. I've got him all to myself now. I can be sad on my own and I don't have to share him with some girlfriend of his who wants me out of the house. Louise got his car, but I bet she doesn't even think about him anymore. I bet she sold the car. But I got the tapes. I got all his blues."

I wanted to ask if she missed her first husband—Martinez's biological dad—but I decided to skip it. I don't even know the guy's name. I know that he was a photographer and that they met in Atlanta and that Taleesa had a spoken-word-poetry act and that this was somehow involved in the breakup. I know that there were posters and magazine articles about her spoken-word act, and she burned them all before she moved to Houmahatchee. And I realize now that she was still doing spoken-word routines when I was little, with just me and Martinez as an audience. She'd rap about putting on socks as she helped Martinez get dressed. When we read storybooks, she would make up her own stories about what was on the page. Clifford was a Big Red Monster, she said, because anything that grows too fast is a monster. Clifford had to go live on an island, like Godzilla and Son of Godzilla, because when you grow really fast you develop all sorts of desires and urges that Emily Elizabeth and your other friends don't understand and can't live with. That's all I know about Taleesa's first marriage. I'm still not sure whether Taleesa or her husband is the Big Red Monster.

Grownups like Taleesa and Dad are lucky. They lost somebody, and they found somebody else. Some people, you know, have lots of chances for true love. I knew in my heart that I wasn't that kind of person. I don't click with most of the people I meet, male or female. I'd had love—in the form of a cute boy's number—and I had lost it. And I had to find it again.

"What's the chance that someone else is going to the fair twice in a weekend?" I asked Taleesa as we pulled up to the fairground.

"Would this someone be a blond-haired boy in a red flannel shirt?" Taleesa asked. I said nothing. "If he's part of one of those contests—the model cars on display, the fancy chickens and all that—I'd say your chances are pretty high."

"You're right," I said. "Let's go there, to the pavilion where all the animals are on display, and see if we can find him. On the way to Elizabeth."

"Forget that," Martinez said. "I'm not going to the fair just to look for some dumb boy and then spy on an elephant. I'm going to Fall to My Death."

"We'll split up," Taleesa said. "Martinez and I will go spend some tickets. You go look for your friend. And then we'll meet up at the elephant ride and get to work."

It was far too hot for my hat. I carried it in my pocket anyway. As soon as Martinez and Taleesa were out of sight, down the row of funnel-cake stands and dart-throwing games and then around the corner, I took the hat out and put it on. I couldn't take a chance on Emory not recognizing me.

I headed into the pavilion, where there weren't as many animals in cages as there had been the day before. The calf that had been in the corral by the entrance, clean and shiny and sweet-smelling, was gone, and so was the big blue first-place ribbon that had been hanging on the corral fence. There were empty spots on the tables between the model cars and planes, a sign that some of the contestants had taken their cars home. The ones left behind didn't look so great, and I felt unreasonably sad for those cars, abandoned by people who never put a lot of care into building them, people who saw no point in keeping a car that didn't win an award. I sighed again, and searched the crowd for Emory's face.

"You never called me," said a voice behind me.

I turned and there he was. If I had imagined the scene in a dream, it wouldn't have been better. Same crooked smile, same shock of coarse blondish hair, same red flannel shirt, but with a darker-colored T-shirt underneath it today. The light in the room seemed to grow brighter as I took in a deep, excited breath. Love is supposed to be about your heart, but for me, it's all in the lungs, in deep breaths that I can't control.

"I thought you liked me," he said, sounding confident instead of hurt. "You didn't call."

I stepped up to him and tugged at his lapel a little. "I told you I'd lose the number if you gave it to me that way, and I did," I said. "But look, we found each other anyway."

Emory shrugged. "I thought this was the right place to look," he said. "I figured if you had a model or a giant pumpkin or something on display, you might come back to get it. So you made a model car?"

"I'm more into animals," I said.

"Let me guess," he said. "A cute little piggie?"

I shook my head. My hand was still on his lapel. "I was thinking more about bears," I said. "Stuffed bears."

"That's it," he said. "Give me your phone. No, really, give it to me."

I am a smart young woman. Far too smart to just hand someone my phone. *Love is such a strange thing*, I thought, as I fished out the phone and gave it to him.

"There," he said. "I've started a text, to my number. Now. Send me a text, so I'll have your number."

I should have typed out TEST. But I'm crazy.

atticustpeale: I'm in love with you. Are you in love with me? Yes/no.

I put my phone back in my pocket and we just stood there beaming at each other. I heard my text make a dinging sound in his pocket.

"Aren't you going to read the text?" I asked.

He didn't break eye contact with me. "What does it say?"

"It says something important," I said.

"I know what I want it to say," he said. "I hope it's that."

"What do you want it to say?" I asked.

"What did it say?" he asked.

"Are we flirting again?" I said. "Is this all flirting?"

"Yes," he said. "And you're doing it fine. So, what does your text say, that's so important? Just say it."

"Just dig in your pocket and read it," I said.

"Are you asking permission to do something?" he asked. "Is that what's in the text?"

"In a way," I said. "Maybe."

"Well, I'm giving you permission," he said.

"To what?" I said.

"To kiss me," he said. "I give my consent."

"Oh, really?" I said. "You think I'm asking permission to kiss you."

"I hope you are," he said.

"Well, I'm not asking consent," I said. "I'm giving it. I'm giving you consent to kiss me."

He grabbed my hand in his rough hand. And he put another on my side, just above my waist. And he did it. We did it. Kissing really is a little weird and slimy, but it's all the other things you expected it would be, too. Part of me wanted to point one foot up in the air like you see in the movies when a girl has her first kiss. Another part felt like neither foot was touching the ground.

"You kids stop that!" said a high-pitched voice. We both turned to see an old white lady, someone I'd never seen before in my life.

"You ought to be ashamed, doing that here," she said. "There's little kids here. I should tell y'all's parents what y'all are up to."

Emory turned to me. "Let's get out of here."

And we ran, hand in hand, out of the pavilion and into the dark night lit by carousel lights.

▮ ▮ ▮

If I tell you I ran off into the dark with a boy, you'll think there was a lot more kissing that went on. And you'd be right.

But if I told you I can't tell you the full story of what happened out there—at the edges of the fairground, where darkness meets light—you'd probably think there was way more than just kissing going on. That's the way people think. People think that as soon as the lights go out, the pants come off.

But that's not how it was. There was kissing. There was hand-holding, both of his hands in both of mine, as we stood face-to-face, breathing together. And there was something that *happened.* There was some kind of magic, magic that nobody looking from outside could have seen. Magic from just standing there and staring at each other in the dark. I don't want to talk about it, because thinking too much about it could turn the magical into the mundane.

I'm sighing again, now, just thinking about this.

Frankly I don't know what was said, and what was just in my mind. Did I tell him a hundred times that I loved him, or did I simply think it, loudly, at the top of my lungs?

I do know that it was speaking out loud that brought it to an end.

"Your arms are so strong," I said. "Your hands are so rough. Not like a lot of kids our age."

He didn't say anything. He kissed me again.

"You're almost like a person from another time," I said. "I mean, you even wear a watch. Who wears a watch who isn't a grandfather?"

He grinned. "Well, I have responsibilities," he said.

Then, reflexively I guess, he looked at the watch, and our moment came to an end.

"Oh, no," Emory said. "Oh man, oh no. Look, I have to go. I have something I have to do and I'm very late."

"Oh no," I said. "Is your family going to leave or something?"

"Something like that," Emory said. And he stepped back. "Look, you have my number now. So really call me. Call me this time."

"I will," I said. "But you never answered my last text."

"What was in your text?" he said, beginning to back away.

"Read it," I said.

"What did it say?" he said, walking away now, and talking louder.

"I love you," I said. "It said that I love you."

"WHAT?" he shouted, and I realized he was toying with me.

"I SAID I LOVE YOU," I shouted.

"I know," he said. "I just wanted to make you shout it."

"DO YOU LOVE ME?" I shouted. He turned as if he didn't hear, and kept walking.

And then he turned, and put his hand beside his mouth, and shouted, though it was almost impossible to hear over the fairground sounds.

"Yes!" he said. And then he turned and walked away, much faster.

▮ ▮ ▮

My mind was racing with a hundred ideas. His watch, like something a grandfather would wear. For a moment I seriously entertained the idea that he was literally an old man in a kid's body—a charming handsome vampire who was actually a hundred years old, or a Captain America-type hero, frozen in time. Utterly illogical, I know, but just then I was beginning to realize that I was in love and was loved back, like the star of any movie. When you're in love it's easy to feel that the script of the world was written with you as the main character. If aliens come to earth, surely you're the one they'll contact. There's a soundtrack. Real violins play. The music swells when I think about kissing him. Surely everyone else can hear it.

"Get back to your work, Atty," I told myself, as I started back toward the lights of the fair. As I walked, I felt taller than I had before. I felt like a girl with long legs and a big stride. I'd come to the fair as a little troll-girl and now that someone loved me I was just like those ladies from the Hallmark movies with the Stormy Kromer hats: tall, confident, athletic. This is what being in love is, I decided. You can go back to your normal life and do normal things, but now you ride on some sort of cushion of joy.

Walking between the rows of booths at the fair—big strides!—I smiled and waved at people I didn't know, as if I were famous, and they waved back. I passed a line of nervous people waiting for Fall to Your Death. I passed the Elizabeth Tavoris booth and the World's Smallest Woman trailer, where there were no lines. I walked past a real circus tent, where someone opened the flap for a moment and in the warm light I saw a woman in a frilly bathing suit juggling something. Next to the tent was the big sign for ELIZABETH III, QUEEN OF THE ELEPHANTS, but I couldn't get close enough to the corral just yet because the entrance was completely blocked by a knot of tall, long-haired girls maybe a year or two older than me. Well, they looked a year or two *taller* than me, but they were giggling like sixth graders.

"Would you?" said one of them to another.

"I would," the other girl said. "He's *hot*."

"He's just a kid," another girl said. "He's like a seventh-grader or something. And his hair is like dirty, and his hands."

"But he's got swagger," said the first girl. "I don't know, he's confident. Look in his eyes."

I shook my head, but with a smile. Love! I remembered that pudgy guy at the fair earlier, the one with the safari hat. It was neat and funny to think that these girls had the hots for him. He wasn't handsome and he certainly wasn't younger than these girls, but love will make you think all kinds of things.

"Excuse me, ladies, are you in line?" I asked, and they parted in front of me, still giggling.

And that's when I saw it.

Yes, Safari Hat guy was there again, still with the safari hat, taking tickets and holding what looked like a black cane with a silver handle. Elizabeth was still in the corral in the dim light, looking bored and sad as she walked around her little circle with a mom and two kids on her back. But I knew, instantly, that it wasn't Safari Hat guy that these girls had been giggling about.

I knew because Emory was there.

He was in the corral. He was leading Elizabeth the Elephant on a rope. And holding, in the other hand, a slim little stick, like the riding crop that you see English foxhunters carrying on TV.

"Emory!" I shouted. "What are you doing in there?" But I knew. I knew, instantly, why he was there.

Emory finished his walk around the corral, handed the rope to Safari Hat Man, and held up one finger, as if to say, "just one second." Then he came over to the edge of the corral, near me.

"I should have told you," he said. "This is why I had to leave. This is why I'm at the fair every night. This is my elephant. Well, this is our elephant, my family's elephant. This is our work."

I didn't know what to say. Elizabeth's sad eye rolled around and focused on me. *If you are who you say you are . . .*

"You're mad," Emory said.

"I'm not mad," I said. "I don't know, I don't know what I'm feeling."

"I didn't flirt with them," he said. "There are always girls like this. I'm just doing my job, and there's always someone who giggles like this. I talk to them just like I'd talk to any customer. They never buy a ticket."

I turned back and looked at the girls. One of them looked ready to burst into tears because I was talking to Emory. Another was either filming us, taking a photo, or reading her phone in a very pointed, I-am-ignoring-you kind of way.

"Look," Emory said. "I'll be glad to let you ride. You don't even need a ticket. You can have Elizabeth all to yourself. Because you're my girlfriend. I mean, you are my girlfriend, aren't you?"

I looked at Emory, and then I looked at Elizabeth. She regarded me for a second, and then looked elsewhere, as if she'd given up hope. She'd decided I was a just another one of the girls who come to the fence and sigh at Emory. I guess that was a thing. And I looked at the tired mom sitting on Elizabeth's back. Safari Hat Guy helped her off the elephant and down the stairs of the platform next to the corral. The mom's two sons were already at ground level. One of them was talking to himself and punching imaginary bad guys.

And I just turned and ran. I ran away in tears.

▮ ▮ ▮

"If you know a boy is doing something wrong, is it okay to be in a relationship with him in the hopes that you'll change him?" I asked Taleesa.

"No," Taleesa said. "That's a hard no."

I guess I knew already what that answer would be. I didn't ask until just before bed, when Taleesa and I were folding towels fresh out of the dryer and Dad and Martinez were hogging the bathroom with pre-bed tooth-brushing.

"I shouldn't have asked," I said. "Now you're judging me."

"Who am I to judge?" she said. "I mean, I married a white man. Men aren't us. They're men. They're usually from a different place, from some screwed-up family or some not-screwed-up-enough family. They're different. There's always going to be some difference. You've got to ask yourself whether it's a difference you're going to put up with. Obviously if a guy steals from you or cheats, you have to leave. You can't count on people to change. You can't expect it. But if the problem is, like, he just whistles too much or chews too loud—well, that's a judgment call."

That's when I told Taleesa the whole story. Well, minus some kissing, maybe, but the basics. I told her that the boy I love is one of the people who were forcing Elizabeth to work.

"That's bad," Taleesa said. "That's really not good."

"I just thought that, maybe, if I stay with him, if we stay together, maybe I can convince him to see things my way," I said. "I feel like he's the only person who understands me, I said. Surely he can understand this part of me."

Taleesa just shook her head. She looked like she was about to say something, but then she went back to folding clothes.

"I know," I said. "This is not me. I'm not the kind of girl who says these things. You must be wondering what got into me."

Taleesa shrugged.

"Not really," she said. "Sounds to me like you're in love. End of the day, it'll probably pass. Most of the time it does."

"And when it doesn't pass, that's when you know it's true love," I said.

Taleesa shrugged again.

"It's a lot more complicated than you know," she said. "If I told you ten times a day that you were my one true daughter, you'd start wondering why I need to say that. I don't tell you that. I don't think about who's a true daughter or whatever. I just wash your underwear and make you clean the dishes and drive you to school. True love isn't a thing you get, it's a thing you do."

"But that's not the same as, like, the love between you and Dad," I said.

Again, the shrug. "Maybe," Taleesa said.

"Okay," I said. "At least tell me that it's possible to love somebody until they change. I mean, if Dad was always riding around on elephants, you could make him come down, right?"

"Oh, hell, yes," Taleesa said. "I can keep him from being a fool. But I don't know that I can keep a man from *wanting* to be a fool. Look, is there more to this than you and your elephant-keeper? Are you worried about us fighting? Is that what this is about?"

"You and Dad are fighting?" I asked.

"We're in disagreement about something," Taleesa said. "We wanted to settle it between us, because when y'all kids find out it'll just be that much tougher to argue."

"Well, now I really am worried." I said. "You have to tell me."

"Your dad's thinking about becoming a judge," Taleesa said.

I chuckled. "Come on," I said. "He's a Democrat."

Most of the judges in Alabama are elected. And they run for office as Republicans or Democrats. That may seem strange, because if a person's job is to be fair to everybody, they shouldn't have to run as a member of one party or the other, but that's the way it usually is. And we all know which party you have to be in to get elected in Strudwick County.

"He's thinking about becoming a city judge," Taleesa said. "You know, someone who puts on robes every Wednesday and goes down to City Hall to rule on cases about traffic tickets and public intoxication and all those little things that never make it to district court. Those judges don't have to run for office. They get hired by the city council, and they can stay on for years."

"That's so weird," I said. "Dad as a judge. Why would he want to do that?"

"It's steady money," she said. "I mean, they get paid well and they always have work. We don't tell you and Martinez this, but the work we do isn't easy. I'm always hunting for writing gigs. He's always scrounging for clients. It's hard. And your dad is getting older. I think he'd like to have an easier life. Honestly, I think he'd like to have a title, like Judge Peale."

"But you don't like it," I said.

"I just can't," Taleesa said. "I married a man who gets people out of prisons. I know he'll never be a prosecutor—someone who charges people with crimes and has them sent to jail. And I guess I knew that if I married a lawyer, I could wind up as the wife of a judge. I just never realized that I really don't like judges. I really don't like the whole system, including judges, and I didn't realize how much this kind of thing would bother me. To live in this tiny Alabama town and to be a part of the system in that way . . . I'm struggling with it." She laughed a little. "And I'm also struggling with the fact that I really *do* like the idea of at least one of us getting a regular, stable paycheck."

I felt off-balance. It had never occurred to me that money was such a problem for Dad and Taleesa. Everyone thought we were rich. Historic house, fancy-sounding jobs, Dad's suits and ties. I always thought Dad drove a beat-up old Hyundai because he wanted to be humble. Taleesa always bought gas $5 or $10 at a time, and she always joked about how this was just instinct when you're a poor person. I thought she was talking about an instinct from the past.

"This is a lot," I said. "Why didn't you tell us all this before?"

"Honest truth? I don't need to hear from Martinez on this right now," Taleesa said. "I'm proud of his imagination and enthusiasm, but you know what he'll do."

I laughed. "He'll look up 'judge' on the internet and come up with a thousand privileges and titles Dad should use," I said.

"He still wants me to say 'admiral on the bridge' every time he comes into the kitchen," Taleesa said.

"And then he'll look deeper and he'll see all the terrible things judges did back in slavery times, and he'll start begging Dad to beat up the other judges," I said.

"I wouldn't put it past him," Taleesa said.

"Well, we're in the same boat, then," I said. "We're both in love with somebody we need to change. Somebody we need to convince."

Again the shrug.

"I don't know if it's quite the same, but I won't argue," she said. "Let me ask you this: how would you feel if you were Emory, and you found out that Atty was going out with you hoping you'd change? Or I'll put it another way: what if you found out that Reagan, this whole time, had been hanging out with you just so she can convert you to her religion? I know she's not doing that, but how would you feel if she did? That's another thing to consider in this whole thing: not just what's right for you, but what's right for the other person."

❚ ❚ ❚

I lay awake that night thinking about what Taleesa said. I knew Reagan was my true friend. I knew she wasn't there just to "witness" to me or win me over to her church. Still, she had asked me a couple of times to come to church with her. And there were a couple of times, talking on the phone late at night or in the bleachers in the ballgame, when she got full-on preachy about the blood of Jesus Christ and all that. I know she believes what she believes, and I admire that. When she asks me to go somewhere, particularly when she's excited about it, I want to go just because she's there. But somehow, when she asked me about church, it never seemed like a deal between me and Reagan alone. I got the feeling that I was being asked by a whole family of people.

If I'm honest, I didn't want to see Reagan in this other place, with other friends and with people who mean a lot to her. Maybe there's a close friend, a Born-Again Atty, who she holds hands with at church. I'm not inclined to share her, and I don't need to know about anyone else who's in her life.

I can see why Reagan wants to witness to me. I can see why Reagan wants to get me into Heaven. I mean, if you were headed there, you'd really want a friend with you. Heaven scares me as much as death. It scares me as much as just vanishing. I mean, can you imagine life in a big resort where you never see Earth again and you're just deliriously happy all the time? There's something creepy about it. I never met my mom, but it's weird to think of her and my grandmother and Old Martinez sitting in a restaurant in Heaven City saying *isn't this food just great*? And *isn't everything great? I'm just so happy*? And not talking about anything else? Not knowing or caring what happens on Earth? Creepy.

I do feel a little better, for some reason, when I hear stories of people who were briefly dead. You know, people who had a heart attack, and then their heart stopped, and then the doctors got them restarted. These people always say they heard a loud noise, and then started speeding down a long tunnel toward a light and heard beautiful loud music and eventually wound up at a place where they felt warm and loved. It's nice to think that this is what's waiting at the end of life, even if it's just something you feel when your brain is dying or something that happens because they've pumped you full of drugs.

Sometimes when I pass a cemetery, it makes me feel better to think that maybe all those people are down there with their dead brains, still feeling warm and loved. Maybe the dead-brain feeling goes on after you die. Maybe that's why skeletons always seem so unreasonably happy, dancing with hats and canes at Halloween, laughing way too loud—laughing like someone who has decided they can't go on. They're like mysterious celebrities. Whenever someone finds a skeleton, the skeleton is immediately famous. Everybody wants to know more about the skeleton, but the skeleton is saying nothing. Even if the skeleton is three thousand years old, the voices on television want to know its secrets.

Once you're a skeleton, there's no downside to fame.

I I I

I really do not have time for school.

I have a love life. I have an elephant to save. I have a no-kill shelter to create. I stay up until the early-morning hours thinking about skeletons. It's no wonder I struggle with algebra.

"You kissed a boy before I kissed a boy," Reagan said at lunch. "How is this possible? You're half a lesbian."

"Sister, I am a whole lesbian," I said. "And a whole, well, whatever a not-lesbian is. I am two whole ladies. And one of them is getting kissed."

Reagan shook her head. "This can't be," she said. "Those are my lines. I'm the one who's large and contains multitudes."

"Get used to it," I said. "I'm the hot one today. You're the sidekick."

"Just today," she said.

"I'll take it," I said. "It's the best day. And it's the worst day."

"Because of the elephant thing," Reagan said.

"Elizabeth," I said. "Elizabeth's not just a thing. Elizabeth has a mind. I can see it. I know it in my gut—just like I know I'm in love."

"Well, what on earth are you going to do?" she said. "Sounds like this elephant is Emory's family business. If you free Elizabeth, you can't expect him to still like you."

"I know," I said. "I can't . . . Oh, wait, my phone is buzzing." I took it out and showed it to Reagan. A ringing phone with the name EMORY on the screen. "Look at me," I sang. "A real boy is calling me!"

We both knew I couldn't pick up. Houmahatchee High's cell phone policy is full of all sorts of loopholes. Teachers don't mind you looking at your phone, but if any sound comes out of it, you're in big trouble. If you put the phone to your ear you can be sure a teacher will take it away. Purple Devils Don't Make Phone Calls.

"How is he able to call in the middle of school like this?" Reagan asked.

"I don't think he goes to school," I said. "I think he's home-schooled. He travels with the carnival and studies on his own. He's smart, and he's in this weird situation, and he's very grown up. He's like a male Reagan Royall."

"Well, that's definitely sexy," Reagan said.

The ringing stopped and we both sat there, staring at the phone.

"I can't believe we're both sitting here waiting for a boy to text," Reagan said. "Are we that uncool?"

"Yes?" I said.

Ding.

> **Emorymahout:** You are the only girl I care about. There are always girls at the fair who giggle at me. I didn't do anything to lead them on. Please don't hold this against me.

"So that's his last name, Mahout?" Reagan asked.

"I doubt it," I said. "I think that's a word for a guy who rides on an elephant. Like, the word they use in India."

"Sounds kinda racist," Reagan said.

"Maybe," I said. "Or maybe that's what an elephant-keeper is called in English, too. I mean, do you know what the English word is for someone who keeps elephants?"

"So what's his last name? Do you even know?" Reagan said. "And what about THIS?" She picked up the phone and pointed to the text.

"Don't," I said. "Don't mess anything up. Don't touch the phone. I need to think about what to say next."

"*We* need to think about what to say next," Reagan said.

"I don't know," I said. "I mean, he's texting me. Me personally. He has a right to think he's having a conversation only with me."

"Oh, come on," Reagan said, still holding the phone. "Every guy who texts a girl knows that he's talking to more than one person. Girls share their texts and talk about them. Everyone knows this. Besides, you need me to help. I am chaos. You need the chaos I bring."

I wanted to say that maybe I'm the chaos now, that maybe

I'm the one who can bring her own chaos. I mean, I kissed a boy first. I'm the chaos leader at this point.

I was actually going to say these things, but just as I opened my mouth, there was a fantastic crash in the lunchroom. Of course, there are always crashes, with some kid dropping all his food and then slinking back to the lunch line in embarrassment. But this was different: a senior, not looking where he was going, walked right into a lunchroom worker who was pushing a stack of clean plates through the lunchroom on a cart. The crash was *loud.* Everybody stood up to get a good look and figure out what caused this commotion.

Everybody but Reagan, that is.

When I sat back down, she was just finishing a text.

On my phone.

"There," she said, placing the phone gingerly back down on the table.

I scowled at Reagan and leaned over to look at the screen.

Atticustpeale: What's your last name?

"What?" I asked. "That's our response?"

"It seems like something you'd need to know," Reagan said. "Both for your own personal safety and if you're trying to take his family to court. And it's chaos. It'll throw him off balance."

"It has nothing to do with what he's texting me about," I said.

"I know," Reagan said. "Chaos. Mystery. It'll keep him on edge."

"I don't think I like this way of communicating," I said. "Life is hard enough when everybody is honest about what they want."

"Look, he's responding," Reagan said. Sure enough, we were seeing the little dots you see on the screen when the other person is typing. But then they stopped. And no message appeared.

"He's having second thoughts about telling you his name," Reagan said. "That's strange. What could that be about?"

"It could be about anything," I said. "I'll ask him when I call him after school."

"No! You can't call him!" Reagan said. "You have to go back to the fair."

"Why would I have to do that?" I said.

"Because of the Rule of Three," Reagan said. "You know. In riddles and in stories, things always happen three times. In jokes, things always happen three times. There's some kind of magic in doing things three times. You've been to the fair twice in two days. If you want magic to happen, you've got to go back and see him again in the same place. Third time's the charm."

"I don't think it works that way," I said. "There's not a rule of three in reality. It's just something storytellers need to make a story work."

"Magic doesn't happen for you because you don't believe," Reagan said. "You have to believe what the World's Smallest Woman tells you. You have to believe that Elizabeth Tavoris is a famous actress. Just go with the magic for once in your life."

▮ ▮ ▮

None of my teachers knew anything about my relationship with Emory, but I couldn't help but think they were somehow against the idea of me seeing him again, because every teacher seemed determined to assign as much work as possible. Thirty problems in algebra. A whole chapter to read in physical science. A reminder from the health teacher that our nutritional journal—a week-long catalogue of everything we eat and its nutritional context—was due Wednesday. I hadn't done any of the journals, so I realized I had just two days to remember or make up multiple days of past meals.

Part of me had been counting on that assignment to be cancelled because of widespread rebellion against the whole project. A couple of kids said their parents would call the school and protest because the food-tracking thing would hurt kids with eating disorders. (I was shocked and delighted to see that Peyton Vebelstadt, who never took a stand on anything, was adamant about this issue. Peyton with a backbone!) One kid even said he was opposed to the federal food pyramid: he asked if he could use his own Alabama Food Pyramid, which included a Pig group, a Greens group, and a Puddin' group.

Reagan was livid about the teacher's demand that we list the number of potato chips eaten every day.

"Who came up with this, the Pringles company?" she asked. "Chips aren't all the same size. If you break a chip you have two chips. If you break those two, you've got four. If you get down to the dust at the bottom of the bag, you've eaten infinite potato chips."

"That's why you don't eat the dust," I said. "Infinite calories."

Even so, the number of tasks on my schedule was expanding like the calories in potato-chip dust. I hadn't worked on the twenty-year animal shelter plan in days. I had to count calories, for this school assignment. There was a new pair of drumsticks, which Taleesa ordered only after much begging from me, sitting unopened on the dining-room table. Easy was mad about sharing the bed with a giant stuffed bear, and I knew he'd need a walk and some attention as soon as I got home. And now I had to go back to the fair for a third night and make magic happen.

As the health teacher droned on about good and bad cholesterol, I felt a vibration from the phone in my pocket. A text. Emory's last name, just waiting for me to read. I didn't even have time to fish my phone out of my pocket until the bell rang and we all headed to the car-rider line to be taken home.

Emorymahout: Mumbford. Not a typo. The B is silent.

Emorymahout: Do you still like me yes/no? :)

Emorymahout: ???

"How would I even pronounce the 'B' in Mumbford," I said to no one in particular, as I waited among the car-riding kids.

Dad pulled up. For the first time I noticed that Taleesa was right about his car. His Hyundai looked tiny and old compared to the rumbling Jeeps and pickups.

"What's this about a boy?" he said as I got in.

"What's this about being a judge?" I said.

"Taleesa told you," he said.

"Taleesa told you," I said.

He shook his head. "Martinez," he said.

"Martinez doesn't know anything about a boy," I said.

"Sometimes his guesses are very good," Dad said. "So tell me about the boy. I'm fine with it. I mean, as long as everything is fine."

I told him everything except the kissing. I think it's the first time I ever kept something from him without feeling bad about it. As long as I'm not breaking some kind of rule, I figure, who I kiss is my business.

"What is this Emory's last name?" he said.

"Mumbford with a 'B' except the 'B' is silent," I said.

"How would I even pronounce the 'B' in that?" Dad asked. "Mumford. Mumb. Ford."

"I know, right?" I said. "So now it's your turn. Judge Peale. What's up with that?"

"Please don't go around saying 'judge,'" he said. "It's far from a done deal. I've got to meet with all sorts of city officials and answer all kinds of questions—and I don't even know that I want to do it."

"I don't see you as a judge," I said. "I always saw you as the guy who gets people freed from jail."

"Or tries to get them free, and fails, more often than not," Dad said.

"But not the person who sends them to jail," I said.

"Well, there's not a lot of sending-to-jail in city court," Dad said. "It's mostly fines."

"And then when people don't pay the fines, where do you send them?" I asked.

"Fair enough," Dad said. "But I've got my bills to pay, our bills. And, I mean, it's not a dishonorable thing to be a judge. It's more money. It's the way people get ahead in our system."

"I think that's what has Taleesa upset," I said. "I think she always saw you as someone who's against the system."

Dad was quiet for a while.

"That's a deep question for me," he said. "My whole life, I've been looking for ways to stay in Alabama without giving up my principles. That's why I settled on being a defense lawyer. There's always going to be somebody who's poor and out of luck and in trouble with the law, and that person's always going to need someone to help them out. And it's something you can make a living at, if you work hard. But I guess I always thought that maybe one day I'd move up to something else. I really felt that any job in the system, if you do it honestly, is a good job. You've got to believe in the legal system in order to be a lawyer, Atty. And I do."

"I'm hearing a 'but' somewhere," I said.

"Well, Taleesa's never had that faith in the system that I've had," Dad said. "And I see why. It's clear that her dad was set back quite a bit by some bogus, small-time arrests and convictions that had everything to do with driving or walking around a mostly white city as a Black man. I know this in my head—the fact that a lot of people don't believe in the system—and I've known it for a long time. But it's been really strange to be so close to someone who has such a completely different view of all this. It's strange to see a little of it through her eyes. It's strange to me to look in her eyes and see that she's disappointed in the idea that I'd be a judge. It's strange to me that I understand why she's disappointed. And it's strange that we're both open to taking the job anyway."

"Sounds like you don't really want it," I said.

"I don't know what I want," Dad said. "What I know is that my current job is a lot of work for not a lot of money, and I'm feeling burned out. And you never hear about a burned-out judge. Speaking of overwork—I've got to stop at the courthouse to pick up some paperwork. Hope you don't mind."

"I don't," I said. "I need to stop in and see Backsley Graddoch anyway. Being friends with the county attorney may have its advantages. I'm hoping he can help me pull up some records on the people who run the county fair."

Graddoch has at least three offices—one at the County Commission Building, one in an office building he owns on the town square and another at his big mansion of a house. If you want to find him, though, the best place to try is the courthouse, even when he's not arguing a case. He always jokes that that's what a lawyer really is: just someone who hangs around at a courthouse.

"Long time no see," said the deputy as we went through the metal detector. "Working on a big case?"

"Maybe," I said. "Seen Backsley Graddoch today? Is he here?"

"Courtroom 2A, if they haven't let out already," the deputy said. "The judge would probably rather you wait outside instead of going in."

So while Dad ran off to do his work, I plopped down on a bench outside Courtroom 2A.

Now, if you've been to courthouses a lot, you know there are a lot of people there in orange jumpsuits, and they're people who are in court because they're about to go on trial. I've seen a lot of people call them "criminals" and say that it's scary to share the hallways with them, but you're not a criminal until a jury says you are. And people aren't scary when they're in handcuffs with a deputy standing right over them. They're just sad and quiet. They actually cry sometimes.

So that's why I was surprised, when I sat down, at the reaction I got from the lady who sat across from me. She was in an orange jumpsuit, with chains on her wrists and ankles, and she smiled broadly when she saw me, the way the folks at the nursing home smile when the animal shelter brings around dogs for them to pet.

"Hey!" the lady whispered, like she was passing a note in school.

"Hey," I said. I stood up and extended a hand. "I'm Atty."

Before shaking my hand, the woman looked up to the deputy standing next to her.

"I can shake her hand, can't I?" she said, again in a whispery voice. "I'm not dangerous."

The deputy nodded. "I know, Lindsey," he said. "Go ahead."

"I'm Lindsey," she said. She stood up, a little stooped from the chains on her wrists, and shook my hand. Actually, neither of us stood all the way up. We just shook and sat right back down.

She had an interesting face. Lindsey was white, and at least in her forties—ladies in jail always look a little older than they really are—but her eyes sparkled with some kind of girlish mischief.

"You're really young," Lindsey said. "Are you here for a custody case? Adoption?"

"I'm doing research," I said.

"Oh," Lindsey said. "School."

"Actually, I'm snooping on a boy," I said. "I'm snooping on a boy I like."

Lindsey sighed. She sounded the way I sound when I sigh over Emory.

"When I was your age, I was just boy crazy," Lindsey said. "You should snoop on them first, though. Some of them are dangerous."

"This is what all the adults tell me," I said. "Every time I tell someone I'm in love, they're all like, wait a minute, love isn't all that real, people are dangerous, and all that."

Lindsey shook her head. "You won't hear me telling anyone to stay away from love," she said. "I'm still as boy-crazy as ever. Being in love is the best feeling in the world and don't let anyone tell you otherwise. It's why we're put here, to be in love. You can't live without it."

I giggled. That was weird. That's not me. But it felt good.

"Boys will disappoint you sometimes, but you have to believe," Lindsey said. "Believe in love. Believe in your dream."

Just then, the door to the courtroom opened and people began filing out—including Backsley Graddoch, struggling with an arm full of papers, and Sheriff Troy, who motioned to Lindsey and the deputy.

"Come on, Lindsey, it's your turn." he said. Lindsey stood up and shuffled down the hall toward the courtroom with the deputy at her side. Graddoch looked up and saw me.

"Hello, the Peales," he said, waving and looking past me, down the hall. That's when I noticed Dad, apparently done with his errand and headed down the hall toward me. Graddoch approached us both and put his free hand up to the side of his mouth like someone sharing a secret.

"So that's the shotgun lady," Graddoch said, quietly.

"I don't know this one," Dad said.

Graddoch waited for Lindsey and the cops to enter the courtroom, out of sight.

"Shot her boyfriend," Graddoch said. "Puts the body in the back of a pickup to drive him, well, who-knows-where. And we don't know where because she passes a deputy who sees the boyfriend's arm just flopping out the back of the truck."

"She didn't close the tailgate?" Dad asked. "Didn't get him all the way in?"

"Big fella, I reckon," Graddoch said. "So the deputy pulls her over, and she gets out of the truck—*shotgun in hand.* And she shoots the dead boyfriend one more time. And drops her gun, and surrenders."

"Good lord," Dad said. "That lady hates her boyfriend *and* her lawyer."

"Allegedly," I said. I guess my voice sounded a little dark. The conversation stopped for a few seconds.

"Why do so many people kill people they love?" I asked.

"Sweetie," Dad said. "I imagine the relationship was already in pretty bad shape by the time this thing happened."

"Oh, I don't know," Graddoch said. "I think loving and killing goes together pretty often. I'm not saying it makes sense, but I've seen it. If nothing else, you kill your husband or best friend or uncle because they're right there. Most people kill people who are close to them. It would be rude to kill a stranger."

All of a sudden I felt a little sick. It's not like I was flashing back to that time I got shot at myself. I mean, it wasn't a flashback like in the movies, where you're there again, at the scene of the Bad Thing That Happened. Still, I felt sick and unsafe like I did back when the Bad Thing happened.

"We've gone too far, Backsley," Dad said. "Atty, are you okay? You look a little green."

I nodded, short of breath. By which I meant that I was okay and that I was a little green. If you've ever seen a war movie or disaster flick, you know that "okay" is a relative condition. In an emergency, if you can say you're okay, you're by definition okay. As for looking or feeling green, I was starting to feel that maybe this was a permanent change. The older and more grown-up I get, the more queasy I feel, all the time.

▮ ▮ ▮

I must have looked more panicky than I realized, because Graddoch was sweet to me for about a half-hour after that. He, Dad and I went across the street to the County Commission Building, where Graddoch set me up in a big comfy chair in his office and told his secretary to bring me a Coke and copies of all the paperwork on Mumbford

Entertainment, the company that Emory's parents owned. The county fairground belongs to Strudwick County's government, so every business that operates at the fairground has to file paperwork with the county.

"I can tell you right now: you won't find a legal argument to shut them down," Graddoch said. "I've already had a close look at their paperwork, and I feel like I've got a pretty good legal mind."

"Good Lord," I said. "They own a transfer truck. And it says here that they paid more than a quarter of a million dollars for it."

"Hell, they probably paid a hundred thousand for the elephant," Graddoch said. "Here's the long and the short of it. The federal government has rules about who can and can't keep an elephant in captivity. There are regular inspections, and all that. It's not cheap. You've got to provide all sorts of medical care, a big, sturdy shelter, five acres or so of land for the animal to walk around in, and so on. That includes a fairly roomy trailer, if you're transporting the elephant. Expensive."

"If you're the size of an elephant, riding in a tractor-trailer would be like me riding to school in the trunk of Dad's car," I said. "It doesn't sound very humane."

Graddoch shrugged. "Even a zoo's going to have to take a pachyderm to the doctor at some point, so you have to have rules," he said. "And maybe those rules weren't made for people who transport an elephant several times a year—but, you know, circuses have to operate somehow."

"Maybe they do," I said. "Maybe they could just make do with clowns and jugglers and leave elephants alone."

"True," Graddoch said. "I have my own lawyerly problems with performing elephants, but the law is what it is. So . . . the Mumbfords have a ranch in Dixie County, Florida. And you'll see that they've got paperwork out the wazoo from Florida. They've got Florida permits that let them travel to county fairs and offer these rides. And they've been popping across the state line to our county fair, on and off, for quite some time. Before I was county attorney, in fact."

"I don't see a lot of Alabama paperwork here," I said.

"Alabama doesn't have a lot of rules about this," Graddoch said. "If there's no rule on how to transport an elephant for display, I guess you could argue that it's not really legal to transport an elephant for display in Alabama. Personally, I'd rather not have an elephant here—because if something goes wrong, if somebody gets trampled, they might sue the county—but the problem is that this was already going on before I took this job. If I tell the Mumbfords they have to go away, without offering some kind of legal rationale, they're almost certain to sue the county for denying them a business opportunity."

I sighed. Lawsuits, money, business opportunities, no mention of whether the elephant is suffering. I always have to remind myself that Alabama law wasn't really written for animals.

"Have you met the Mumbfords personally?" I asked.

"Can't say I have," Graddoch said.

"Well, I'd like to meet them," Dad said. "At least, there's one member of the family that I think I really should meet."

CHAPTER FIVE

◇

Martinez didn't know it, but he felt the same way I did about the Rule of Three.

"Even I don't want to go to the fair for a third night in a row," he said as we walked Easy that afternoon. "If you keep going again and again, there's no magic."

Taleesa didn't want to go either. So after walking Easy and grabbing a sandwich, Dad and I headed off to the fair.

The county fair is a different place on a Monday night. There's still blaring music, still twirling rides, still the smell of funnel cakes. What's missing are the young couples holding hands, the crowds of teenagers and the sense of mischief in the air. Instead, you see grandparents leading groups of kindergartners around. You see the occasional bored-looking middle-aged couple who just saw the fair from the highway and stopped to take a look.

In the elephant corral, Elizabeth paced in circles, with no one on her back, led by the guy with the safari hat. I knew now that Safari Hat Guy was probably Russell Mumbford, Emory's much-older brother. Emory leaned against a fencepost, also looking bored. A couple of grandpa-and-grandkid groups stood watching, but they didn't seem interested in anything more than a look at an elephant. There were no high school girls, with their beautiful long hair and Instagram-ready fashions. High school girls were home doing homework, I assumed. No one was here to giggle at Emory today, no one but me.

"I know you want to meet him," I told Dad. "But let me talk to him first."

Emory's face lit up when he saw me, which brought out a tumble of emotions in me. A cute boy whose face lights up for me, of all people! I felt a moment of joy, and a real dread of the conversation that had to come next.

"Atty!" he said. "I'm so glad to see you. So you forgive me for all the stuff those girls said?"

I smiled in spite of myself. "There's nothing to forgive," I said.

He hoisted himself up a little on the fence, and leaned over toward me. "In that case, I'm giving you consent," he said.

I laughed. "I'm not going to kiss you right here in front of all these people," I said. "That's my dad right there. No, don't wave."

"I've been waiting all day to see you," he said. "I really thought I lost you."

I took a deep breath.

"Look," I said. "There's no easy way to do this, but I don't want to be like some lying girl in a romantic comedy. I need to tell you who I am."

"Atticus Peale, dog lawyer?" he said.

I wasn't expecting that.

"More or less," I said. "Yeah. How did you come up with—"

"The very first time we met, you made some comment about how local people know who you are," he said. "Once I had more of your name, I Googled you."

"And you're not . . . upset?" I said.

"Of course not," he said. "We're so alike. You love animals and I love animals. You spend your time taking care of dogs and cats and I spend my time taking care of Elizabeth. You want to meet her? Let me introduce you to Elizabeth." He turned to the guy in the safari hat, but didn't raise his voice. "Russell. Bring her here."

Russell and Elizabeth kept on pacing around the corral until they came near us and stopped. This close, I suddenly felt how big Elizabeth was, how unusual it was to be so close to such a giant creature. Still, I wasn't afraid at all. Her eye, the one I could see, seemed sad, afraid, resigned. She wasn't going to hurt anybody, but she wasn't happy.

"Good girl," Emory said, patting her leg roughly. "Atty, meet my other girlfriend, Elizabeth. Elizabeth, eat her hat."

Yes, I was wearing the Stormy Kromer hat again. Elizabeth swung up her big, rough trunk, grabbed my hat softly, pretended to put it in her mouth, then placed it back, sloppily, on my head. People behind me laughed. It didn't seem like Elizabeth was having that much fun. Elizabeth looked distracted, like someone at a desk, rubber-stamping papers.

"Isn't she great?" Emory said, beaming. "Somehow, when I met you, Atty, I just knew you were an animal lover too."

I laughed. "My friend Reagan says I smell like someone who sleeps with a dog," I said. "Maybe that tipped you off."

"Well, I guess I smell like an elephant, or like hay or whatever," he said.

"I don't think Mama and Deddy would want you to talk to her," said Russell. "She's one of those animal activists."

Russell was an interesting person to look at. Short and stocky, with a flat face, he wasn't just wearing a safari hat, but a specific kind of safari hat—one that was a little pointy, like something an old-fashioned British soldier would wear. And with it, leather sandals, cargo shorts and a sweaty short-sleeved white dress shirt that was half-untucked.

"She's fine," Emory said, turning to look at his brother. "She gets me. She understands."

Russell shook his head. "You know how this goes," he said. "These animal activists, they'll do anything to sneak up on you and film you or whatever. Mama and Deddy already told you not to talk to her. And who's that guy with her, in the suit? A lawyer? A politician?"

"That's my dad," I said. "And he is a lawyer, but it's not necessarily what it looks like."

"Just stop, Russell," Emory said.

"If it's not what it looks like," Russell said, staring me down, "then what is it?"

I was speechless for a minute. What, indeed, is it?

Emory grabbed my hand. "It's love," he said. "That's what it is."

I put my free hand to my mouth for a second, with tears coming into my eyes.

"Emory," I said. "I am in love. But he's right about something. I am here because of Elizabeth."

He pulled his hand back. The look in his eye told me a lot about his life. I knew, just then, that I was not the first person who'd told him they were disturbed by Elizabeth's situation. I could tell that not everyone Emory met believed that life with the carnival was neat. I could tell that Emory often met people who thought his life was weird, and those people told him so. The look in his eye was the look of someone who's used to people making an ugly face at him when he tells them who he is. I know that feeling.

"I'm sorry," I said. "Look, I met you before I knew you were involved with the elephant. The whole reason my family keeps coming back to the fair is that they're worried about Elizabeth. Worried that she's not happy here."

The look on his face made my heart break.

"So you came back to see Elizabeth, not to find me," he said.

"Both," I said. "It's complicated. I—"

"Goodbye, Atty," Emory said. "Elizabeth doesn't need you to worry about whether she's happy. She can do fine without you. We can do fine without you."

In elementary school, I saw a boy cry once because he didn't want to go to the bathroom. Houmahatchee Elementary was in an old building and it was in pretty bad shape, and I'm told there were no doors on the boys' bathroom stalls. I saw another boy cry when Santa visited one year and brought us all mini-Squishmallows. You can only buy the minis in sets of six, and there were 19 of us in the class, and Santa did the math wrong, leaving one boy without a toy when everything was handed out. These Squishmallow and bathroom tears were real tears, like you'd cry at a funeral.

You don't see teenage boys crying nearly as often, particularly when it's over hurt feelings. They tend to shout insults instead. But crying is exactly what Emory did. He turned his back to me, still standing next to Elizabeth, and cried like a kid without a Squishmallow.

God, I love this boy so much.

I opened my mouth, but nothing came out.

"You need to go," Russell said. "Elizabeth is happy. And Emory is happier without you."

I scowled at Russell. "That's for Emory to decide," I said. "And come to think of it, that's for Elizabeth to decide. Why would she be happy here riding people around on her back?"

"You don't know what it was like!" Emory shouted. He turned to face me again. "Before we bought her, she was in a petting zoo! She lived her whole life in a cage no bigger than the truck we drive her around in! She had scars on her knees and on her side from being stuck in that cage!"

"That's terrible," I said. "But she wasn't born in a cage, was she? At some point, she lived out in the wild with other elephants. Does she live with other elephants now?"

"She came to the petting zoo as a baby," Emory said.

"A baby from where?" I asked. "Where was her mom? Where was her dad? Who is she, really? Who *is* Elizabeth?"

"I don't know," he said. "She's from somewhere in Asia. India, or Thailand maybe. But I didn't take her from her parents. We didn't take her from her parents. We're giving her a better life. Look her in the eye and tell me she's not happy."

I shook my head. "I'm so sorry," I said. "But that's not what I see. When I look in her eye, I see someone who was stolen from her parents. I see someone who's lonely."

"Well, a lot of people are lonely," Emory said, wiping his nose. "Maybe there are worse things in the world. Maybe we'd all better get used to being lonely."

Russell: "You need to go, now, girl."

Emory: "He's right. We're done. You need to go."

❚ ❚ ❚

Ever seen the movie *Dumbo*? There's a scene where storks are flying out of Heaven to deliver babies to their mommies, and one stork spirals down to meet a circus train that is chugging its way across a map of Florida. If you look closely to see where the stork meets the train, it's right about where Dixie County would be. Dixie County, the place where Emory's family has its elephant ranch, home to a single elephant: Elizabeth.

Dumbo's mother and a bunch of other elephants are riding in a single train car when the stork arrives and sings "Happy Birthday" to Jumbo Jr. And then they unwrap the bundle, and we see that Jumbo Jr. has *giant ears*. And the other elephants make fun of Jumbo Jr.—they call him "Dumbo" and they shun him. But Dumbo goes off with his mom and is happy, for a while.

It hurts to be shunned. But what about an elephant who doesn't have any other elephants around them at all? No mom to cuddle him? How does that elephant feel? If you'd never had humans around you, since the age of maybe four or five, how would you feel? How would you even know what you feel? What words would you know, to allow you to describe your feelings?

If you look up elephants on the internet, that's one of the auto-fills that comes up. "Do elephants have feelings?" This happens when you look up dogs and cats, too. I wonder sometimes about the people who are doing these searches. Who's this person who really wonders if dogs or elephants have feelings? I can understand why people would wonder about oysters or snails, but who listens to a purring cat and wonders if cats have emotions? Who hears a chihuahua barking and wonders if the anger is real? What else would cause that behavior? A bunch of wheels and pulleys in the little dog's head?

When people ask if animals have emotions, they're asking *are they like us*? And are they like us in ways that matter?

Here's what I know about elephants, from the stuff I've read so far. There's a story about a mahout—yeah, that's the word for an elephant driver in India. A mahout was working with elephants to move big logs around. There was one elephant who had his trunk wrapped around a big log and the mahout tried to get the elephant to drop the log in a hole. The elephant refused. And when the mahout looked in the hole, there was a little dog sleeping there. As soon as the dog was shooed away, the elephant plopped the logs right into the hole.

You don't act that way if your head is full of nothing but wheels and pulleys.

A woman in Kenya found an elephant that had been shot by poachers. The elephant who had been shot was dying, but two other elephants propped their bodies against her, trying to keep her standing up.

They say that when elephants come across the bones of long-gone elephants, they stop and caress them, maybe because they're taking their time to think about the life that's gone.

Almost every time you hear a story about the bravery or kindness of elephants, it's a story in which the elephant dies, shot by a human. If you knew only these stories, you'd wonder if humans were intelligent and had feelings. You wouldn't wonder about elephants.

But humans do have feelings. We love elephants. We love them to death. That's why Dumbo and his mother are on a train. We want to touch elephants, to ride them, to see them stand on their hind legs under a circus tent. Some people say there never would have been zoos in America without elephants, because the elephant is what people really want to see. The elephant is the act that draws the crowds. And because we love them so much, we've sometimes forced them to live with shackles on their feet, or in tiny cages, or all alone, with no one else of their kind to talk to.

Sometimes we love them like Lindsey loved her boyfriend. Why do we always hurt people we love? Isn't there some other way?

❚ ❚ ❚

It's tough to wake up in the morning and know that you had true love for all of three days. And you screwed it up. And now you have a whole future life to go through, maybe seventy years, without feeling that way again. And on top of that, you have to go to school at 7:30 without your math homework done.

There's only one thing to do when you're washed up at thirteen. Put in the earpods and get out those new drumsticks. If you look around the classic soul lists on the internet, you'll never run short of songs about people who ruined their lives by losing their one true love. "Kiss and Say Goodbye," by The Manhattans. "After the Laughter," by Wendy Rene. You can record a song that will live forever and still be a loser who screwed up your one true chance at love.

I was right in the middle of "Misty Blue" by Dorothy Moore when Martinez burst into the room.

"I wish you would stop that drumming and howling," Martinez said. "You're driving me crazy. And anyway, it's cultural appropriation."

"YOU DON'T EVEN KNOW WHAT I'M PLAYING," I shouted. "I HAVE EARPODS IN."

"It's soul," Martinez said. "It's blues. I can tell by the look in your eyes. And they're my drums."

"IT'S NOT CULTURAL APPROPRIATION IF I'M NOT PLAYING FOR AN AUDIENCE," I said. "I DON'T WANT AN AUDIENCE. I WANT YOU TO GO AWAY."

He kept it up on the car ride to school.

"They're my drums," he said.

"Martinez, just let it go," Taleesa said. "Ah, crap. We have to stop for gas. All this driving to and from the fairground."

Did you know that compared to men, women are twice as likely to catch fire while pumping gas? Martinez saw this on the news years ago, and he quotes it every time we pull into Chevron. He's been jockeying for years for the chance to pump gas like a grownup, and Taleesa never agrees. I feel like I'm old enough to pump, but Taleesa always sends me into the store with her card because—maybe 20 years ago—some dumb store owner accused her of stealing gas. You always get the receipt, she says, and make sure you look the clerk in the eye.

"Ten dollars on Pump Two," I said to the lady behind the counter.

Counter Lady looked surprised.

"Who is Elizabeth?" she said. "I can't believe it. Who is Elizabeth?"

I didn't have words.

"What?" I asked.

"You're the Who-Is-Elizabeth Girl," she said. "The one from Facebook. I told Chelsea that the video was from the fair HERE and she didn't believe me. Can I get a selfie with you?"

"I have no idea what you're talking about," I said. But then I had a sinking feeling that I did.

"It's you, I know," she said. "In the video on Facebook. You're crying and you're arguing with your boyfriend and he's standing right next to the elephant. You had you a boggin on."

"It's a Stormy Kromer cap," I said.

"Well, I just want you to know I'm on your side," she said. "It's sad about the boy and all, but I think they should set that elephant free."

This is bad, I thought. This is very, very bad.

And it *was* bad. There was indeed something on Facebook. A grandma at the fair had been recording video of

Elizbeth around the same time Emory and I began to raise our voices. The grandma got almost all of the argument on video—with cuts to Elizabeth at key moments, where you could see the look in her eye. The video's title on Facebook: "WHO IS ELIZABETH?! TEEN DRAMA AT THE STRUDWICK COUNTY FAIR."

It had 12,456 views and 598 likes followed by a long line of emojis. It was actually shot really well, but it was painful to watch. Did I really cry, so obviously, throughout this whole argument?

"I told you the hat was a mistake," Reagan said as we watched the video at lunch. By then, the views had crossed the fifty-thousand mark. Luckily, nobody else at school seemed to have seen the video. I mean, who uses Facebook in high school?

The comments were awful and stupid, because comments are always awful and stupid. Yes, people commented on the hat. A bunch of angry-sounding guys said I seemed like another Greta Thunberg, which should have been a compliment, but for them it wasn't. Some folks said it was obvious I was "on the spectrum." Clearly they didn't know what a spectrum is. Aren't we all on it, by definition?

And of course there were always the "fat" comments. I couldn't believe that those were there, because I was actually in a skinny phase. I don't know how things work for you, but I tend to get kind of roly-poly for a couple of months, then I grow noticeably taller over a few months, then I get roly-poly again. In the video, I was Taller Atty.

"This is so typical of guys on the internet," Reagan said. "There's a pudgy guy in the video with his shirttail hanging out. There's a literal elephant in the video. And out of all that, they find the little girl and say she's the one who's fat."

There were also plenty of people who were on my side in the elephant debate, though some of them also seemed confused. Someone in Atlanta kept asking where this fair was so she could boycott it. Obviously, if you don't know where the fair is, you weren't planning to go anyway, so you can't very well boycott it. When someone posted the location of the fairground, some other person on the internet accused them of doxxing me—not Emory—by letting the world know where the fair was. "I know who this girl is and I'm not going to let you threaten her by allowing her to be identified," this person wrote. So weird. I mean, I've already been shot at. I've been on TV in a turkey costume. A former governor of Alabama put out a press release full of lies about me. And now my lover's quarrel is all over the internet. I think I don't have a lot to lose by telling you that I live at 922 Burnt Corn Creek Road, Houmahatchee, Alabama.

Given all the views the video was getting, I thought about posting a link to the Strudwick County Animal Shelter's website, in hopes it would attract some out-of-town pet parents or donors, but I decided to stay out of the conversation. There were people on the site saying mean things about Emory, too. And there were people calling for a protest at the county fair later that day. I didn't want to look like I was egging them on.

I texted Emory before the lunch period was over.

atticustpeale: I'm so sorry, Emory.

It didn't take him long to respond.

Emorymahout: What are you sorry FOR?

I typed a response and erased it. And I typed another one and erased it. What *was* I sorry for, really? I wasn't sorry I told him the truth. I wasn't sorry I wanted Elizabeth to go free. I wasn't sorry for being who I am and I wasn't sorry for being in love with Emory and I wasn't sorry for kissing him. I felt terrible about all the online stuff, but I wasn't the one who posted it. I was sorry the way you say you're sorry when someone's grandmother dies.

I tried to text him a couple of additional times that day. Every time, I erased the text before sending. Part of me hoped he was watching on the other end. Seeing the little dots that showed I was typing. Hoping a message would come through.

❚ ❚ ❚

It rained all afternoon and into the night on Tuesday. A TV reporter came all the way up from Pensacola to see if there were protests against the elephant rides, but all she found was a soggy ghost-town of a carnival. Nobody wants a wet funnel cake, and you can't Fall to Your Death in the rain. None of the rides were running.

Emory and his family weren't there. They'd packed up Elizabeth some time that morning and headed back to Florida. Protests, for the most part, didn't happen. The reporter found one older woman who drove all the way from Cape San Blas to stand in the rain with a posterboard that read "Who Is Elizabeth?"

"Well it's definitely a load off my mind," Backsley Graddoch said the next day. "I really do think that elephant ride is a disaster waiting to happen. Some idiot throws a firecracker at the elephant, or it steps on a broken bottle or something and suddenly it goes into a rage and people are dead and everyone's asking why the county allows it. Personally I hope they never come back to Strudwick County again."

"Maybe your problem is solved," I said. "But Elizabeth's problem isn't. I'm sure she's still on that truck, getting hauled all over Florida. She's not free."

And that wasn't the only thing that was unresolved. Would I ever see Emory again? And if I did, what could I possibly say? Think hard, Atty!

And while I thought, I got back to my normal, abnormal life. Meeting with Graddoch to work on the twenty-year animal shelter plan, going to the shelter to help Megg clean enclosures and walk the dogs. Actually doing homework at home, instead of cramming it all in during homeroom and getting obvious stuff wrong. Lying on my bed with Easy, the only person I know who sighs as much as I do. Did Easy have a long-lost love, too? Is that why he heaved a big sigh every time we relaxed together like this?

"What if we're as bad as the elephant-ride people?" I asked Megg one afternoon, as we cleaned the kennels in the always-stinky animal shelter. "I mean, we're keeping dogs in cages just like they keep Elizabeth cooped up. We literally kill dogs if they don't find a home. Every dog looks sad when you close them up behind bars, no matter how good it is for them in there. What if some girl came in there and said: 'the look in this dog's eyes tells me she's not happy here.'"

Megg didn't miss a beat.

"I don't think we're one thing like them," she said. "First of all, if someone wants to take one of these dogs out of the shelter and give him a home, we'll let them. We'll be glad. That's what we're here for. Second, we're not here to make money. Even though we charge some money for an adoption, you know we go to the county commission for help every year because the adoption fee never brings in enough to cover the expenses. And that's fine: we're not here to get rich, we're here to help. Most of the big arguments we have are ones that revolve around *who* we're here to help. Are we here to make life better for humans in Strudwick County or are we here to make life better for animals? But we never, ever sit down and ask how we're going to get richer off these animals. What do you think Emory's family would be doing with Elizabeth if making money weren't the goal?"

I thought for a minute.

"Well, they seem to have some kind of zoo-like operation in Florida," I said. "And I don't know, maybe that's good. With enough room, an elephant can eat hay and walk around and live in peace. You could even allow a few visitors in, but you wouldn't want to force Elizabeth to come up to where they are so she could see them."

"And you wouldn't be loading her up on a trailer and carting her around so people could ride on her back, would you?" Megg said.

"No," I said. "There's nothing in it for her."

▮ ▮ ▮

I was home that night, lying in bed with Easy and my math homework and my worries, when my phone rang. I couldn't believe who it was.

"Hey, Emory," I said. It was quiet on the other end. "Hello?" I said again.

"Atty, can we talk?" Emory said. "I've had a bad day and I just need someone to talk to. Can we pretend there's no Elizabeth and we never had an argument? And just talk?"

My sigh probably sounded like one of exasperation, but it wasn't. I couldn't think of anything I wanted more than to talk to Emory as if nothing happened. "Absolutely we can talk. What's going on? What's wrong?"

"Some of it . . . some of it's hard to explain," Emory said. "I don't know. Do you have an older brother? An older sister?"

"Martinez is my only brother," I said. "He's a couple of years younger than me."

"Well, Russell is my brother, but he's a *lot* older," Emory said. "And he's kind of like a third parent. My folks let him boss me around, and they always have. And when that's good, it's good. I mean, he sticks up for me. But when it's bad, it's bad. I'm the only kid here, really, and when everybody's criticizing me, it's tough."

The way he said it, I wondered how many people were included in "everybody."

Years ago, Taleesa took me with her for a magazine interview with a girl who was starting her career in stock car racing. As it turns out, that girl inherited her stock car from her dad, who had also been a racer. When we went out to the house for the interview, it seemed liked everyone in the family—grandma, cousin, and so on—was in the racing business, and they all seemed to live together in the same big house. It was easy to picture Emory in a similar situation.

"All this trouble you're having, is this about me?" I asked. "I didn't know anyone was going to make a video. I didn't mean to hurt you."

"That's just part of it," Emory said. "It's just Russell. When we lose business, it shakes him up. He starts thinking about what we'd all do for a living if we didn't have Elizabeth. So he's always coming up to me and asking 'what are you going to do when this elephant dies?' And if I say I'll just get some other job he gets mad and tells me I'm disloyal. But if I say I don't know what I'll do he gets mad and starts ranting about how I don't have any future. No matter how I answer, I'm wrong, and he's mad."

I thought for a minute.

"Maybe Russell's mad at himself," I said. "I mean, he's in, what, his twenties, and he works for his parents? Maybe he feels stuck, and he's mad about that."

"Oh, he doesn't just feel stuck, he *is* stuck," Emory said. "And I am too. But knowing why he's saying this stuff doesn't make it any easier. Look, Atty, I just want to talk to someone, someone I like, about something that isn't me being stuck. Look, you love animals and I love animals. Tell me what your favorite animal is. And you can't say 'elephant.' Or 'dog' or 'cat' because that's too easy."

When I was little, I would give Taleesa constant Favorite Animal updates, because my favorite changed roughly once every 1.27 days. Why was it so hard to think of one now?

"I think my favorite animal is the one we haven't met yet," I said. "I think there are animals on other planets. Other star systems. I want to know what they look like."

"I think sandhill cranes are my favorite right now," Emory said. "You'll be working outside, and you'll hear that honking sound, and there they are, flying overhead. It's nice that there's something beautiful out there that can surprise you. What's your least favorite animal?"

That took no thought at all. "There are certain kinds of jellyfish that are immortal," I said. "They don't age, really, and I guess they can live until some fish eats them. For some reason, the idea of living forever, but without knowing or learning anything, creeps me out. The only thing that scares me more is death."

It went on like that, for a long time. We talked about our favorite movies—we both liked *Ponyo* when we were little—and about what our rooms looked like. I learned that homeschooling was hard, and that, except for his days on the road with the carnival, Emory didn't see a lot of people outside his family. Emory was sweet in ways that no boy in school ever seemed to be. He still had most of the stuffed animals from his elementary school days. Even though he didn't play with them, he couldn't bring himself to put them away. I told him about my toy squirrel McNutters, who lives in a dollhouse in the corner of my room even now. I don't play with McNutters much anymore, but he's still in there, drinking martinis and soaking in his hot tub.

For that moment, I was like a girl with a really good boyfriend. It was good. And then the conversation came back around to Russell.

"You know, I don't think Russell's ever had a girlfriend," Emory said. "He gets mad when girls giggle at me, like they did the other day. He gets mad when girls giggle at him, even though that doesn't happen a lot. I feel like he's mad a lot of the time. Maybe you're right that he's mad about being stuck."

"He's not stuck, though, really, is he?" I said. "He could leave home. He's old enough. Just get a job and leave."

"It's not that easy, I think," Emory said. "Where would he go? Who would he live with? He knows one thing—this elephant—really well, and I guess that's the only job he knows how to do."

"When you put it that way, he sounds a little bit like a prisoner," I said.

"It's not a prison, just a family," Emory said. "We've all got a house and a neighborhood we can't leave, because where would we go, right? And it's not a bad place, it's just that you can't leave."

"But you can, Emory," I said. "I mean, not now, but when you're grown up."

"Maybe," he said.

"Yes," I said. "Yes you can. My stepmother did that. She couldn't stand living with her dad's girlfriend and so when she left high school she picked up and went all the way from Milwaukee to Atlanta on her own. Now she's a writer. If you're miserable enough where you are, you can do it."

"You don't understand what it's really like to be stuck," Emory said. "You've got a lot more options than most people, I think. Your parents let you do all kinds of things, all this lawyer and activist stuff. You don't know being stuck."

That hurt. I didn't say anything, because I didn't know what to say. Emory shouldn't have said anything else, either. But he kept on talking.

"That's why you're wrong about Elizabeth," Emory said. "She's in the same situation. You want her to be free, but what does 'free' mean? What's she going to do, just roam around Florida looking for food? She's a member of our family, and she needs her family to keep her alive."

I couldn't stop myself.

"She *had* a family," I said. "Nature gave her a family. Somewhere. In Thailand, or India maybe. And somebody took her away from that family. Most of the stories I've read about elephants, baby elephants taken into captivity, they get captured after someone kills their entire family right in front of them. And now she lives without a single elephant around her. How long has it been like that?"

"Well, *we* didn't capture her in the wild," Emory said. "We took her in because she was working in a much worse place. And you don't know that she got captured as a baby. You don't know that."

"But she probably did get captured in the wild as a baby," I said. "That's how it usually happens, because grown elephants are a lot harder to ship overseas. Emory, has it ever occurred to you that Russell's unhappiness is a lot like Elizabeth's unhappiness? Don't you think she feels like a prisoner? Don't you think she feels stuck?"

"How do you know?" he said. "How do you know? Why do you get to be the voice of animals all of a sudden?"

"It's the same every time: I wind up speaking for animals because no one else will," I said.

"This call was a mistake," he said. "Atty, I love you but I really don't like you."

He hung up before I could say anything else.

CHAPTER SIX

◇

Love is hard on everybody.

Take Martinez, for instance. Not long after our adventure at the fair, Houmahatchee played Jacksonville High School in football. And in the crowd from Jacksonville was a tall, pretty girl named Fallon, who was probably three grades ahead of Martinez. That didn't stop Martinez from asking Fallon to be his girlfriend. She replied that he was too young. And then one of Fallon's friends said Fallon would never date him because he was "nartistic." Fallon told her that was a mean thing to say, and that she should hush, but the damage was already done.

Martinez was stunned. In all these years, no one had ever told him he was nartistic.

"Everything is falling into place now," he said as we were fixing dinner the next day. "All the problems I've had in classes. The way teachers talk to me. It's all because I have narticism."

"I don't think narticism is a thing," Dad said.

"You're a lawyer, not a doctor," Martinez said. "I bet if I told you I had epicormic branching, you'd believe me."

"It's pretty loud at those games," Taleesa said. "Are you sure she didn't say 'narcissistic?'"

"I don't even know what that is," Martinez said.

"It's from Greek mythology," I said. "There was a guy who was so good-looking he sat around looking at his reflection all day in a pond. And he sat there looking at himself until he turned into a plant."

"So this girl is hating on me for being good-looking," Martinez said. "I really can't help that."

"Well, being good-looking is just part of the story," Dad said. "What if she said you're 'not artistic'? Do you think that's maybe what she said?"

"Nah," I said. Everybody who meets Martinez knows he's the creative type. This is the kid who dressed as Batman every day for eighteen months of his life. He even wore a Batman suit under a Superman suit for Halloween. He almost got kicked out of kindergarten for refusing to wear normal civilian clothes; Taleesa had to convince him to adopt an alter ego to protect us all from the Joker. The first thing he'd do when he got home every day was rip open his shirt to reveal the Batman logo under his normal clothes.

For more than a year, I had to carry a fully automatic Nerf blaster around the house with me to fend off Batman attacks. That's how I created my own supervillain, Gun Moll. She's a stereotypical 1920s gangster girlfriend, with a New York accent, a beret, high heels, and a tommy-gun. Her superpower is colorful swearing, which leaves Batman bent over with laughter so she can get away. Gun Moll has a great tagline, but I can't tell you what it is. I mean, what if some little kid picked up this book and read it?

"Nartistic sounds to me like someone who's really creative but also kind of self-absorbed," Taleesa said. "Does that sound like Martinez at all?"

We all just looked around at each other and smiled.

"Well, if he is nartistic, it must run in families," Taleesa said. "I'm pretty sure that narticism broke up my first marriage. Good news is, narticism is worst when you're in your early twenties, but then it starts to wear off. For instance, a nartistic person would just pile the mail up on the counter for a couple of days like someone did here. A nartistic person would wait for someone to read it. But look at me: I'm going to open and read."

"I hate bills," Dad said.

"Here's a letter for both of us, Paul," Taleesa said, opening it. "Oh. Oh, that's interesting. Look." She handed the letter to Dad, who took a look.

"It was good of them to approach us before getting in touch with Atty," Dad said.

"Let me see!" I said, snatching the letter out of his hand.

It was from the Elephant and Primate Intelligence Committee, a bunch of law professors who go to court in animal-related cases. They were always in the news when there was a controversy about a chimp, gorilla, an elephant, or a dolphin—and their basic argument was always the same: these animals have rights, like a person does. If you can recognize that you're the elephant in the mirror with a dot on your forehead, they argue, then you ought to be a person under the law. If you can show mercy to a little dog in a hole who's about to be crushed by a log, you're a person. If you can go to a graveyard and mourn others who are now gone, you're a person. Apparently dolphins and chimps can do similar things.

Whenever I talk about this, I feel like I should put my hands over Easy's ears. I don't know if Easy can do all those things, and I don't know how I'd find out. If he couldn't do them, I wouldn't think of him as any less a person, with any fewer rights. Can you really look your dog in the eye and say he's not a person?

Anyway, Dottie Labisky, the director of EPIC, wanted to talk to Taleesa and Dad and get their permission to talk to me, all with the idea of perhaps getting me to take part in a lawsuit against Emory's family. They wanted to sue the Mumbfords to get Elizabeth moved into a better environment.

"What do you think?" Dad said. "Do you want to do this?"

I sighed.

"This is tough," I said. "I don't want to sue Emory's family. But I know that what's going on with Elizabeth is wrong. Why is this so hard?"

"Why don't we call these EPIC folks and talk about it as a family?" Dad said. "I can put her on speaker, if she picks up, and we can discuss over dinner."

So that's what we did. While we ate, Dad's phone sat in the middle of the table on speaker, and we introduced ourselves to Dottie Labisky.

"First," Labisky said. "Let me say that I'm really impressed with the work you're doing so far. When you're old enough, I think any law school would be delighted to snatch either one of you up, Atty, Martinez."

"Bleah," said Martinez. "Law."

"Martinez has other plans," Taleesa said. "Lots and lots of plans."

"I'm going to be the first person to complete the Talladega 500 on a motorcycle," Martinez said.

"And you, Atty?" Labisky said. "Surely you have some interest in a law career."

"I think I'd like to be a drummer in an all-girl punk band," I said.

Martinez threw a roll at me. "Appropriation!" he said. "They're my drums!"

Labisky laughed. "Well, I'll get right down to brass tacks," she said. "We think Elizabeth's case is a strong one. And I mean, a strong case for the rights of elephants. There's plenty of evidence that elephants have a high level of cognition. That's what we call it, cognition, when you're thinking in a complex way that we once thought only humans did. Elephants know they're elephants, and they know that elephants don't live forever. They know that other creatures around them have thoughts and feelings, too, and they're willing to show those creatures some kindness. To us, this is enough to be a person as defined by law. We're not saying that an elephant has the same rights as a person. But we are saying that this human-like thinking gives an elephant—gives Elizabeth—*some* sort of rights."

We were all silent for a minute. There was an uneasy tension in the air.

"I do see a problem here," Dad said. "How you figure out what those rights are? I mean the elephant can't tell us what she wants. So who decides what her rights are?"

"There's one right that really matters here," Labisky said. "There's one right that could change the way animals are treated in court. That's the right to go to court, and to be treated as a person by the court. I know you all know how things work now: an animal, any animal, doesn't matter at all under the law unless it's someone's property. When you go to court for animals, Atty, you have to convince a judge that *you're* harmed by mistreatment of animals. If Elizabeth can be recognized as a legal person, which could happen in this case, that might open the door to a whole new way of looking at animals under the law."

"That would be big," I said.

Still, that uneasy tension hung in the air.

"Look, I'm just going to say it," Taleesa said. "I see what you mean about elephants, but I can't help but feel a little righteous anger every time someone says this stuff about an animal as a person. This is Alabama. Alabama used to treat Black people as property not so long ago. Three-fifths of a person, that's how we were defined under the Constitution. So I can't help getting a little upset when people start saying an elephant is a person. I'm not saying you're wrong about that. I'm just saying there are a lot of people in Alabama, now, who are not getting their full rights. People who are in prison, or who get shot, and who didn't do anything. And I'd be lying if I said it didn't upset me a little to see an elephant going to the front of the line."

"Every single thing you're saying is true," Labisky said. "It's coming from a place of deep knowledge, and I honor it. I don't think I could even come to you with this pitch if I didn't know that Mr. Peale, for instance, is working full time already in the difficult business of helping human beings secure their rights, as a defense lawyer."

Taleesa looked at Dad knowingly, as if to say *and you want to be a judge.*

Dad cleared his throat a little. "You can call me Paul," he said. "No need for Mr. Peale."

"Mrs. Peale," Labisky said. "I hope I can encourage you to see this as more than an either-or. I'd argue that in places where society is more willing to expand rights—places where the government recognizes a right to health care or education and so on—you typically see better living conditions and more attention to the basic rights of *everybody.* And in places that are stingy about rights—maybe a place where people get really mad about lowering the voting age to sixteen—in those places you find that it's often hard to practice the rights that *do* exist. I realize that my experience isn't your experience, but my hope is that we're all better off any time society decides to be a little more humane."

"Wow," I said. "You could lower the voting age to sixteen? I never thought of that. That would be great!"

"There's a lot that courts and lawmakers can do when they set their minds to it," Labisky said. "There's a lot of unusual stuff they've already done with the concept of personhood. Atty, did you know that a corporation is a person under American law? Just imagine that I created a cereal called Yabba-Dabba-Doo, a chocolate cereal, let's say, and I put it in a brown box and started selling it . . ."

"Make it a big box," Martinez said. "Cocoa Pebbles, the boxes are way too small."

"You're getting my point, Martinez," Labisky said. "If

I did make a Yabba Dabba Doo cereal, everybody would know I was copying someone else's product. The people who make Cocoa Pebbles could sue me to make me stop. Not the people, really, but the *business*. A corporation can come before the court and make that kind of demand, just like a person can, because it *owns* the rights to Cocoa Pebbles and Fred Flintstone and all that. The corporation didn't create those things. It isn't even a human or a creature with a brain, but it can own those things and it can sue me. In our system, a corporation is a legal person even though it doesn't have a brain or feelings, and, unlike you and me, it can live forever."

"Like a jellyfish," I said.

"Exactly," Labisky said. "And if a jellyfish can have rights before the court, why can't a whale, or a dolphin, or an elephant?"

"It's an interesting argument," Dad said. "I guess I'm wondering what you want to ask Atty to do that will help with all this."

"It's simple, really," Labisky said. "We've done all the lawyerly stuff. We've written the briefs. We'll argue the case. What we really need is someone to be the voice of Elizabeth. Atty, you hit on it exactly when you invited the world to ask who Elizabeth really is. You win a court case by telling a story, and we want you to testify. To tell the jury your story."

"I don't know Elizabeth's story," I said. "I don't know where she's from or how she got here."

"Just tell *your* story," Labisky said. "Just tell the truth. Tell what you saw and what you felt."

Everybody was looking at me. My mind was racing. I thought of an elephant, caressing the bones of a long-gone elephant and thinking sad thoughts. I thought of the first time Emory grabbed my hand, a move that was so unexpected and felt so comfortable.

And then, something occurred to me.

"Wait," I said. "Where is this trial being held?"

"Dixie County, Florida," Labisky said. "It's where the Mumbfords have their farm."

Dad started shaking his head, and then I did too.

"This will never work," I said. "I've read up on this place. It's out in the country. The biggest city there is smaller than Houmahatchee. You're going to get a bunch of local farmers on the jury. There's no way farmers are going to look at an elephant and say she's a person."

"Florida can always surprise you," Labisky said. "A lot of Florida folks really care about ecology, particularly in beach communities. There's a lot of coastline in Dixie County. And farmers can surprise you, too. Maybe they'll be more open-minded than you think."

"I want to win," I said. "I'd love to see more rights for animals in courts—but what I really want to do is see this one elephant, Elizabeth, have a better life. Isn't there another way to make this case?"

"I'll tell you this," Labisky said. "We've done better, so far, than we expected. I think our chances are good. All I'm asking is that you come to the court and tell your truth. And we *are* asking. We won't call you to testify if your heart isn't in it."

Again, all eyes were on me.

"Can I have some time to decide?" I said. "I think this is something I want to do. But I need to think."

▮ ▮ ▮

Maybe "think" isn't the right word. I mean with choices like this, is thinking what we really do?

Think about teen romance novels. Or rom-coms. On TV. The girl always has a choice between two boys, and they both seem pretty desirable. Both of them make her swoon—and they make you, the reader, swoon too. She has to decide. She dreams about a life with one boy and then she dreams about her life with the other, and she has to say yes to one and no to the other. But somehow, it isn't thinking the same way that, I don't know, solving a math problem is thinking. There aren't any rules, like there are in math. In math, you want to know whether the answer to the problem is seven or twelve, but you don't feel like you're already in mourning for twelve the moment you put seven down as the answer. You don't feel like your life will end if the real answer turns out to be nine.

The girls in those books and movies never really make a choice between the boys anyway. Think about it. There's always something that happens that changes the math and makes her decision no decision at all. She almost marries the wrong boy, but then she catches him shoving a little kid and suddenly she just *knows.* But what if both boys are nice? She has to make a choice, and she has to cry every tear that choice causes, and she has to cry them all by herself.

Lying awake about eleven o'clock that night, I decided I needed someone to talk to. So I called someone. I called someone I probably shouldn't have called. If I was planning to testify in the case, there's one person I definitely shouldn't have called.

"H'lo?" said Emory.

"You sound like you were in a deep sleep," I said. "How early do you go to bed?"

"Early," he said. "I have to get up before sunrise to take care of the animals."

It felt so good to hear his voice. I sighed. I know I do this a lot. That's just love.

"So," Emory said. "You're just going to call me and start talking like we never had an argument? That's how you're going to handle that?"

"That's how I do it," I said.

Now he sighed, and it wasn't an exasperated sigh. "Okay," he said.

"I need help," I said. "Today I'm the one having a bad day."

"What kind of help do you need?" he asked.

"I need you to hold my hand," I said. "I need you to hold my hand over the phone."

We sat there for a while, holding hands. Maybe Heaven isn't so scary after all. I think I could sit here for a good long while, alone under the covers, holding hands with a boy in Florida.

"I don't want to say anything and ruin it," Emory said eventually. "But I want you to know I'm still here."

"I was about to say the same thing," I said.

Then, silent heaven again, for a long time. I don't know what got into me. I opened my mouth.

"Emory, who—" I said. I stopped myself before asking, "who is Elizabeth?" Why would I say such a thing at just that moment? "Who are you, Emory?" I said. "Tell me who you are."

He didn't have to think very long.

"I'm the boy who lives in the forest," he said. "I take care of animals. I get up before sunrise and feed the goats and the horses and Elizabeth, not just because I have to, but because I want to be out of the house. I like animals better than I like people. Goats go right for your pocket. They dig right into the pocket of your jacket because you've reached your hand in there before and pulled out some corn. Animals are simple in what they ask you to do.

"There's a hill behind our house, a hill with trees," he continued. "The hill is mine. I used to go up there with my toys and play. There was something about being out there, where you could hear the wind and smell the earth—there was something about that that made it more fun to play, as if my toys were real soldiers fighting in a real jungle, or real scientists looking for real animals. Then I realized I don't need toys. When I'm at the top of my hill, when I can look down through the trees and see Elizabeth down there throwing dirt around with her trunk, I feel like I'm in a big adventure. Being out in the woods, that's the adventure. When I'm out there I feel like I'm the real me.

"The hill is really mine," Emory went on. "My parents have already told us that when they die, Russell will get the house and I'll get the hill. I guess the idea is that empty land is worth a lot of money because you can sell it for someone to build houses on. But I don't want to sell it. This is my place in the world. I've always known it."

As he talked about his life, I started to get a picture of

what the Mumbford farm looked like. An old, two-story house, with air-conditioning units in the windows that hummed in the summer. Most of the year, though, those windows were open. Little lizards, the kind that do pushups and change from green to brown, would scurry across Emory's schoolbooks as he tried to study in the kitchen. Frogs shouted all night. Elizabeth lived in a barn and spent the day wandering around a fenced-in area that she'd worn down with walking—worn down to the point that there was no grass, only dirt. Emory didn't know any other kids, except the girls who leaned over the fence at this carnival or that carnival. He left his green world only when the family went to Walmart, or when they toured across the country with Elizabeth. That other world was mostly gas stations, parking lots, and fairgrounds. Sometimes, when he was supposed to be studying, he'd get out his phone and read all the newspaper stories about how the gas-station world was eating away at the green world.

"The earth is dying, Atty," he said. "That's why I'm going to stay on my hill. I'm not going to sell it. I'm going to let it be green."

"I wish I could see it," I said.

"I wish you could see it," he said.

Quiet, for a moment, again. A perfect moment, a warm and perfect moment. But I just can't keep my mouth shut.

"What happens when—" I started. Then I stopped.

"Go on," he said.

"No," I said. "Never mind."

"No, you started," he said. "Now you have to tell me."

Why did I go on and say it? Why not make something up?

"If you inherit the hill and Russell inherits the house, who inherits . . . the rest?" I said. "The goats, the horses."

"Elizabeth," he said.

"Yes," I said.

"I don't think it will be a thing," he said. "Elizabeth is old, and my parents are not-so-old. She'll be gone by then."

"Wow," I said. "You say it so calmly. I don't think I could talk that way about my dog, Easy."

"Well," he said. "She's my good friend. I'll miss her. But it's also the circle of life, I guess. I mean, look at all the goats. We feed goats and pet them and then we slaughter them and eat them."

I gasped a little.

"How can you do that?" I said. "To a goat you know?"

"It's part of the natural world, Atty," he said. "It's part of how we get back to nature. If we all raised our own food, if we didn't buy stuff from stores all the time, that would help. It's not any meaner than when you buy a hamburger."

"I don't eat meat," I said.

"Come on," he said, with a little edge of frustration in his voice. He didn't say anything else, but it sounded like he didn't believe me.

"I don't—I don't see how you can do that," I said. "How can you raise a goat from a baby to a grownup and then *eat* it? You might as well eat Elizabeth."

"You know that's not the same," he said.

"Why isn't it the same?" I asked. "What is it about Elizabeth that makes her different from those other animals?"

He was quiet for a minute. I waited. I pictured him in the dark in his house, thinking hard. For a brief moment,

I imagined him coming around to my way of thinking. I imagined us agreeing, us meeting, us holding hands, us wandering around his hill together.

I was completely unprepared for what he said next.

"Are you recording me?" he said.

"Wait, what?" I said. "Why would I be recording you?"

"You want me to talk about how Elizabeth is different from other animals," he said. "I'm such an idiot. Russell told me you'd do this. You're part of the lawsuit."

"So you know about the lawsuit," I said.

"So *you* know about the lawsuit," Emory said. "You're working with them. You're just calling me now to pick my brain and get more information about Elizabeth. I'm such an idiot."

"I didn't call you to spy and I'm not part of the lawsuit," I said. "They want me to testify in court. But I haven't said yes. I'm just thinking about it."

"How can you even think about it?" he said. "Oh, I'm so stupid. I talked to you again! I thought you were on my side. And here you are getting ready to talk against my family in court."

"Testifying is just telling your story," I said. "I'm just going to tell them what I saw. The truth and nothing but. Somebody else decides."

"If you were in court, and somebody asked me to testify, and I thought it was bad for you I would keep my mouth shut," Emory said. "You stand behind the people you care about."

"Are you telling me to keep my mouth shut?" I said.

He didn't say anything.

"No boy is going to tell me to shut my mouth," I said. "No man and no woman is ever going to tell me to stay quiet when I see an animal suffering. Elizabeth is suffering. Everybody can see it but you. And I'm not going to shut my mouth about that."

"Well, I'm going to shut mine," Emory said. "I'm not going to sit here and spill my guts to somebody who wants to spy on me and my family. That's it, Atty. You're not going to hear from me again."

He hung up, and I cried myself to sleep.

Chapter Seven

◇

"It's official," Reagan said. "You, too, are large. You contain multitudes. I have ruled. I'm banging my gavel." She slapped her palm on the lunchroom table for effect.

It was true. Ever since my fight with Emory, I was two people, or more than two. I could imagine one future in which I patch things up with Emory and decide to just pretend that the situation with Elizabeth doesn't bother me. And then there was another future in which I save Elizabeth from Emory's family and also destroy everything that Emory really cares about. Each future felt like an alternate reality, in which I was my own evil twin.

"The crazy thing is that everything I love about Emory, really, comes from this whole situation with the elephant," I said. "I love that he loves Elizabeth. I love that he sees himself as someone who takes care of animals instead of, well, *whatever* it is that these boys at this school think of themselves. Take away Elizabeth and you destroy a big part of Emory. You destroy what we most have in common. But then when I look at Elizabeth—who's probably not seen another elephant in twenty years, and who spends her time walking around in little circles—I think of all that's already been destroyed for her."

To make matters worse, everybody was in on my struggle, courtesy of Facebook. There were a couple of girls from higher grades who stopped me in the hallway and complimented me on my choice of boyfriend. Apparently it wasn't just me or a small group of giggling preppy girls who had taken note of Emory.

"I'm starting to realize that Emory is objectively hot," I said in homeroom a couple of days later. "Like, not just hot to me, but hot to lots of people. It's not just personal taste."

Reagan shrugged. "Meh," she said. "Objectively good-looking, maybe. If you can get past the weird-farm-kid look."

I turned to Peyton Vebelstadt, who was intensely studying her history textbook in the next row of desks. I've noticed that Peyton likes to eavesdrop. Sometimes when Reagan says something completely outrageous in homeroom, Peyton will choke back a little laugh, and then she'll pretend it's something funny in the book she's so intensely reading.

"Hey Peyton," I said. "What do you think? Emory, from the county fair. You've seen him on Facebook. Is he objectively hot?"

Peyton pursed her lips in thought. "Mmmm . . . yes," she said. Then she nodded with growing assurance. "Yes. It's weird that he's hot, but yes, he really is."

"Weird hot is the best hot," Reagan said. "Men get old and fat, but weirdness is forever."

"You know, Atty," Peyton said. "I've been wanting to

tell you how brave I think you are. And how right I think you are. This elephant-ride thing, it just breaks my heart. Somebody should do something about it, and of course, that person turns out to be you. But I don't see how you can possibly keep this boy as your boyfriend after all this. Aren't you afraid—I mean, I'd be afraid—that this was your one chance at true love, and you lost it? Aren't you afraid of being lonely?"

"Yes," I said. "Yes, I am afraid of being lonely." I put my finger on my lips for a second, thinking hard. "I've never really thought this out before, but I guess . . . I guess it doesn't matter that I'm *afraid* of being lonely . . . because I know it's wrong to keep Elizabeth in these conditions. Yeah, I think that's it. Right is right, wrong is wrong, and I guess, compared to that, my *fear* isn't really anything that's important."

"And it's just fear," Reagan said. "There are plenty of boys out there. There are plenty of *people* out there for Atty to meet in the future. Atty might be afraid of being alone, but I'm not afraid that she'll be alone. She's a good catch."

"Awww," I said. "That's the nicest thing you've ever said to me."

"Well, you're still the sidekick and I'm still the star of the movie," she said.

"But, y'all," Peyton said. "If you *do* wind up alone, that's real. That really hurts. I'm telling you, Atty, you're being brave."

Reagan tried to cheer me up by constantly referring to Emory as my "ex-lover." This was an inside joke, that started months earlier when we were watching some dumb British show in which a rich lady announced casually to her friends that she had "taken a lover." It seemed to both of us like a tacky thing to say, particularly in such a classy accent.

"Your ex-lov-ah," Reagan would say, in a fancy accent.

"Lov-ah," I'd reply in the same accent. It was fun to say.

It didn't take long until we got carried away with the thing, like a couple of dumb boys with some arm-punching game. Whenever there was a lull in the conversation one of us would say "Lov-ah!" and the other one would shout back the same. Pretty soon we sounded less like fancy British ladies and more like tropical birds calling to each other. There are a few classes where I don't see Reagan, but whenever we passed each other in the hall we'd squawk out to each other.

"Take a new lovah, Mrs. Smythe!" she'd say.

"Lov-ah!" I'd shout.

"Lov-AH!" she'd shout back.

And that's how we wound up in the principal's office. Again.

Ms. St. Stephens read the note from Dr. Dalton, the vice-principal and chief disciplinarian for the school, and shook her head.

"I don't think I understand exactly why you are here," she said.

"That makes two of us," I said. "Well, three, I guess."

"Look," Ms. St. Stephens said. "I don't want to pry into people's lives, I just want to keep things orderly. Are the two of you having some sort of . . . romantic quarrel?"

We laughed.

"Are you sure?" she said. "I mean, Reagan, do you have some sort of feelings for Atty? Is that what's going on?"

"Why am I always the one people think is gay?" she said.

"It's the hair," the principal said.

I nodded. "It's the hair," I said.

"Oh, come on," she said. "You can have good taste, you can wear purple hair and have an avant-garde haircut and still be straight. And you can be queer and be boring. You can even wear a stupid hat."

"Reagan," I said, "I don't think you can just say 'queer' like that. I can say 'queer,' but you can't say 'queer.' That's how queerness works."

"I am not following this at all," Ms. St. Stephens said. "What is going on here? Someone explain to me what is going on."

I held up my hands, and for some reason I felt a need to close my eyes. "Okay, I am bisexual." I opened my eyes after that. "What I mean is that I like boys and girls, both. But I'm not, like, *sexual*. Nothing like that is going on. With anybody."

"Understood," said Ms. St. Stephens.

"And I am very much *not* bisexual," Reagan said. "I like men. And really only some men. Most of them movie stars. In fact, I have a list in my backpack if you—"

"That really will not be necessary, Ms. Royall," the principal said. "Can someone explain to me what all this shouting of 'lover' is about?"

"It's a joke," I said. "It's like a Downton Abbey kind of thing." I shifted to my fancy-lady accent. "Whatevah is a week-end?"

"It's when you take a lov-ah," Reagan said.

"What's strange to me about this is . . ." Ms. St. Stephens

said, letting her voice trail off a bit. "Well, the very first time you both came to my office, many office visits ago, I thought that I kind of asked about whether there was a relationship between the two of you. And I thought both of you assured me that this was, you know, completely impossible."

"Well, it's still impossible," I said. "But I'm a different person than I was back then. Back then, I wasn't interested in any kind of relationship with anybody. And then, something just *hit* me, and I *was* interested. And, you know, I'd give anything to just go back again and be an elementary-school kid who doesn't care about any of this. Being in love is just craziness and pain, and it makes you act like someone who isn't yourself."

Ms. St. Stephens nodded. "That's the first sensible thing I've heard anyone say this week."

For the record, it was Thursday.

Things were quiet for a minute. I decided to say something to fill the silence, in part because I knew that if we were quiet too long, Reagan would shout out our new slogan.

"Ms. St. Stephens," I said. "Isn't this the part where you're supposed to tell us that we're full of raging hormones, and one day those hormones won't be so bad, and things will make more sense and everything will be better?"

"Well," she said. "I'm not going to lie to you." She turned to Reagan with a warm smile. "You know, it's funny. When I was your age, I kept a list of boys I liked, just like you do. And it kept growing and growing. It got to maybe ten pages."

"That's a lot," Reagan said.

The principal looked a little hurt. "Is that a lot?"

"That's a lot," Reagan said.

"Well, ladies," the principal said. "I can't see a lot here that requires discipline. Let me encourage you, if you want to shout the word 'lover,' which is a perfectly reasonable pastime, do so out of school. And here within Houmahatchee High School, please speak to each other in your indoor voices."

"Lov-ah!" Reagan said to me in a stage whisper.

"Lov-ah!" I stage-whispered back.

❚ ❚ ❚

"So you're out," Reagan said in the hallway, when we were supposed to be walking back to our classrooms. "You came out of the closet. See, it was easy."

"I'm telling you, I was never in the closet," I said.

"So you're going to tell everybody now?" Reagan said. "So I can talk about this with other people?"

"Why would you want to talk about my—stuff—with other people?" I asked.

"I mean, your parents," Reagan said. "You should come out to your parents."

I knew what was really going on here. She didn't talk about it a lot, but I knew that deep down inside, she was fascinated by the idea that Dad and Taleesa truly didn't care whether I was gay or straight, and that this had always been the way our family was. It was odd to her, like a trivia question.

Trivia. *Did you know that some ancient cultures had only four or five names for colors?* It's a silly little useless fact, but once you learn that, you can't help but sit around and think about how this worked. When they saw a purple flower, did they call it red or did they call it blue? The question comes up again and again—when you're sitting on the toilet, when you're washing dishes, whenever your mind comes to a rest. I think my situation was like that for Reagan. She couldn't imagine what the world looked like at the Peale house, with all the crayons in our crayon box.

"I don't think there's any coming out to do," I said. "Like I said, I've always had, I don't know, permission to be gay if I want to be. It's not something I have to, you know, say."

Reagan shook her head.

"But don't you think they want to know?" Reagan said. "I mean, just to know?"

I stopped and thought for a minute.

"No," I said. "No, I don't think they would. Really. I mean, that's the way we do things. Dad and Taleesa are very open and fair and tolerant, but, you know, we don't do specifics, I guess. Dad doesn't talk much about my mom. Taleesa doesn't talk much about her first husband. I don't tell dad about Emory. It's just the way we are."

"So you're afraid to tell them," Reagan said. "Because it will upset things somehow."

"Sheesh," I said. "No. I can tell them when it comes up."

"Look, if you're afraid to tell them, I can tell them for you if that makes it easier," she said.

"Go ahead, weirdy," I said.

At least she asked. I mean, we both understand why there's a thing they call the closet. If Reagan wanted to date girls, and if I just went and told her family, I could really mess up her life because her church is pretty anti-gay. This stuff is for a gay person to share when they're ready to share it. People can get seriously hurt.

"So are you out to the school?" Reagan said. "Are you out in class?"

"I mean, I don't know," I said. "Nobody cares but you."

"So I could talk about this with you in front of other people?" she said. "If Peyton hears that you're bisexual, you're okay with that?"

Reagan always knows exactly where to dig.

"Okay," I said. "Maybe I'm not ready for that."

"See," Reagan said. "You were in the closet. You're still a little in the closet."

"No," I said. "It's not like that. It's just, like . . . If a flower's purple, it should just be allowed to be purple. It doesn't need people arguing about whether it's red or blue."

"I don't get it," she said.

I didn't know how else to explain. All I could think of is a jungle, full of flowers and sloths and bright talking birds, all of which no human being has ever seen and described. One day I'll go into that forest and draw those birds, maybe. I'll name their colors. Or maybe I'll let the forest be forest. Not everything that is private is secret. Not everything that is unseen is hidden.

❙ ❙ ❙

Reagan came home with me that night, on one of our many supposed study sessions. It always amazes me that parents really believe you can study alongside your best friend without goofing off. I mean, you didn't do that at school, so why would you do that at home?

At the car-rider's line that evening, Reagan hopped into the back seat with Martinez, while I jumped into the front next to Taleesa, who was on the phone with her editor.

"Martinez," Reagan said. "Your sister is LGBT."

"What kind of LGBT?" Martinez said, not looking up from his video game.

"She likes boys and girls, both," Reagan said.

"Oh, I knew that," Martinez said.

I turned to stare at him. "How could you know that? I don't talk about this stuff with you."

Martinez put his forearm over his forehead in a pretend swoon. "'Oh, I can't get over the royal wedding!'" he gasped. "'The prince and the princess, they're both so *beautiful*!' That's you. Like, at least once a day."

"I do not talk about the royal wedding every day," I said. "Not even every week."

Cars behind us were honking, so Taleesa got off the phone and started driving.

"Mom," Martinez said. "Atty's LGBT."

Taleesa glanced at me with a bemused look.

"What kind of LGBT?" she said.

"She likes boys and girls, both," Martinez said.

"I was aware of this," Taleesa said.

"How?" I said. "How could that possibly be?"

"You came out to me while we were watching that recording of the royal wedding," she said.

"I came out to you?" I said. "I don't think I did. I don't think I even knew I was bi then."

"Well, it seemed like you were coming out," she said. "I don't remember exactly what you said, but I left with the impression that you had come out. Or maybe it was over that Memorial Day, when Naval Academy commencement was on TV. Remember, when we watched *all* of the Naval Academy commencement for some reason?"

What can I say? I like ceremonies. I like people in uniform. And I like it when people wear white. I wish I could have a little crush on a man or a woman in white without people going straight to a word with "sex" right in the middle of it.

"Atty's bi, Mr. Peale," Reagan said while we were making dinner.

Dad looked a little nervous, the way he does when Taleesa asks him about some errand that he forgot to do.

"Okay," he said. "You mean, like, bisexual?"

"Very bi," I said. "But not all that sexual. Can we get a new word for that?"

"Or just stop talking about it?" Martinez said.

Dad still looked worried. Taleesa patted him on the shoulder.

"Don't worry, Paul," she said. "It's not an update. You didn't miss anything new. It's just something we're talking about."

"Thank goodness," Dad said. "I thought I was losing my grip on reality. I was sure we had this conversation before. The royal wedding thing."

I should have been mad at Reagan for being so eager to get into my business, but in the end I wound up feeling sorry for her. During dinner, Martinez started calling her a "snitch" and a "tattletale" for outing me. Normally Dad and Taleesa wouldn't let Martinez be rude to a guest, but I didn't hear them defend her. Instead, they launched into a conversation about all the folks they'd known, back in the day, who got beaten up or kicked out of the house when they came out—or when somebody else outed them. I could see Reagan getting smaller and smaller in her seat, as she realized she'd broken her own Outlaw Code.

After dinner, Reagan and I had the table to ourselves. I really was trying hard to focus on algebra. But it's hard with your best friend right there. Too much to talk about.

"I can't believe your family is so cool with you being all gay and stuff," she said.

"Told ya," I said.

"And they don't mind you hanging out with me, a fellow girl," she said.

"Well, you're straight," I joked. "And you never wear white."

"Nev-ah!" Reagan whispered.

We were quiet for a minute.

"I feel kind of bad about how you list-shamed Ms. St. Stephens," I said. "I mean, who's to say that ten pages of boys is a lot? It's her business. Anyway, ten pages for her is probably five pages for most people. You know, double-spaced with margins and all that."

"Well, I'm an outlaw, and I've barely got a page." Reagan said. "And you, you like both boys and girls. I bet you can't come up with ten pages."

I said nothing.

"Ahh, of course," Reagan said. "You've got ten pages. And it's all just 'Emory Mumbford,' over and over again."

I sighed. "Pretty much. It doesn't change. It doesn't get better."

"Has he called you?" Reagan said.

"No," I said.

"Are you gonna call him?"

"Now that I've agreed to testify in the case, the EPIC lawyers are telling me that I absolutely shouldn't talk to him," I said. "At least until the case is over."

"If he does call you, are you going to pick up anyway?" Reagan asked.

Another sigh.

"I don't know," I said.

▮ ▮ ▮

Weeks passed, and he didn't call. And I resisted the urge to call him.

I'd like to say I was 100 percent committed to Elizabeth and the court case, but that wouldn't be entirely true. One day in late fall, I got a call from an unknown number in Cross City, Florida. That's in Dixie County, where Emory lives. I knew that because I'd read a lot of stuff online about Dixie County, which I guess was my version of doodling a boy's name on the back of a notebook.

I was at the dinner table, doing algebra homework. The phone was face down on the table. It buzzed. I turned it over, and saw that the call was from Cross City.

A second ring.

I knew I shouldn't answer. I knew that if I did it might mess up my testimony in the court case.

A third ring.

If I didn't answer, would he leave a message? If he didn't leave a message was that the end of everything between us? Would it really end here, at the dinner table?

A fourth ring.

I picked it up.

"Hello?" I said. Silence. "Hello?"

"Hi, I'm Louise and I'd like to talk to you about your car's extended warranty—"

Spam. I guess I was safe. And I guess I wasn't safe. If he called, I guess I would answer it, wouldn't I?

CHAPTER EIGHT

◇

"I don't think Emory has any friends," I said one day, in the car on the way to Walmart.

To Taleesa, this probably seemed like it came out of nowhere. I said it weeks after EPIC had asked me not to call him anymore. Court cases take a long time to develop, and it would probably be February before I actually had to testify. I had been trying hard not to talk about Emory. But I was thinking about Emory and Elizabeth all the time.

"Interesting," was all Taleesa said.

"I mean, he doesn't go to school and he travels and works all the time," I said. "How would he make friends? That's why he called me that one time, even though we were fighting. He doesn't have anyone to talk to."

"I still don't think it would be a good idea to call him," Taleesa said.

"I'm not going to," I said. "I'm just thinking. I'm just putting the pieces together."

The handsome boy with the rough hands, who cries in front of crowds and still has stuffed animals in his room.

The thought of him alone in the back of his parents' car, wishing he had someone to talk to, stirred all the emotions I had. It made me love him like a *lov-ah* but also in the way I love a kitten who needs to be bottle-fed.

But who am I to pity Emory, really? When I do a count of my own friends, I come up with exactly one: Reagan. No, it was worse than that. Reagan was right when she said I was her only friend who was an actual kid. I'm closer to Taleesa than any self-respecting teenager should be with her mom, and if I'm honest, Backsley Graddoch is indeed a genuine friend. Not just a work friend. I like talking to him. Our work sessions on the twenty-year plan weren't as chatty as my homework sessions with Reagan, but there were gossipy moments. We knew some of the same people, and they were people I couldn't talk about with the kids at school.

Graddoch was the only person I allowed to address me as "Colonel Peale." I've been trying to shake the colonel thing off for some time now, in part because it's silly, and in part because it brings up bad memories. It goes back to the time I met with then-governor Fischer King and asked him to help save an alligator from being hunted down and killed. King pulled a fast one on me, making an announcement to the press that made it look like I had made a deal with him to allow the hunt to go on—and he told everyone that he'd appointed me an honorary colonel, which is something an Alabama governor actually can do, though the title doesn't really mean anything.

"You know, I was actually a colonel when I was your age," Graddoch said. "But I did it the old-fashioned way. I wrote to the governor and asked. I wrote a letter to George

Wallace, when he was very old and supposedly repentant, and asked for a commission, and he sent me one of those certificates. I didn't make it stick in quite the same way you did, though."

"I would love to make it unstick," I said.

"In Alabama, once you're a colonel in people's minds, you'll always be a colonel," Graddoch said. "Though, technically, I guess, each of us has seen our colonelcy expire. These honorary appointments really last only for the term of the governor who does the appointing."

"I can't believe Fischer King vanished so fast," I said. "One day he's the governor and he's on the news all the time. And then he resigns in shame and you never hear his name again."

"Well, even Alabama voters have their limits," Graddoch said. "They'll put up with you cheating on your wife. And they might even put up with you raising taxes. But they'll never put up with you doing both. And then Miss Luxapallila Magby, of all people, becomes governor."

"Well, she's not married, so I guess cheating won't be a problem," I said. "She can take a lov-ah if she wants to."

"Everybody knows Lucy Magby's not going to do that," Graddoch said. "And they know she's committed to not raising taxes. In fact, she's committed to not doing anything. And that's exactly what Alabama wants: a governor who doesn't do one damn thing. She's perfect for the role."

"Coulda been you," I said.

"I don't need to be governor," Graddoch said. "I can be just as ineffective right here in Houmahatchee."

I think Graddoch values my friendship, just like I value

his. Just before Christmas that year, Dad and I found a *Best of Yacht Rock* CD at Dollar General and we both agreed it would make a great gift for Graddoch. Even with my tiny allowance, it wasn't much of a sacrifice, but Graddoch got genuinely choked up when he opened it. I don't think he even has a way to listen to it. He drives a brand-new electric Porsche with satellite radio.

Still, until Reagan mentioned it, I'd never *thought* of Graddoch as a friend. It's funny how that works. Some people we see all the time and we hardly think about them when they're not around. And then there are people we hardly ever talk to, but we think about them way too much. Our own personal celebrities.

"My whole relationship with Emory was about three days long," I told Graddoch during one of our work sessions. "I added it up one time, and I found out that I've spent about three hours and eleven minutes talking to him, on the phone and in person. Just three hours and eleven minutes. And in about two minutes from now, I will have spent longer than that just on Section Three of this plan."

Graddoch grabbed a page of Section Three and peered at it through his reading glasses.

"Sounds like you love animals at least as much as you love this boy," he said. "The question is, do you love Section Three?"

I shook my head. "It could use some work," I said.

"I agree," he said. "Maybe it could use another three hours of rewriting. I have to say, though, that you're a fine legal draftsman, for someone who hasn't been to law school. Notice that I didn't say 'for your age,' because that's silly. Lots of kids are strong writers and most adults can't complete three grammatical sentences in a row."

"Well, *you're* pretty good at it," I said.

Graddoch sighed. "I wonder what your mother would think if she saw us working together like this," he said.

"Taleesa thinks it's great," I said. "I think she respects you for working on the Jethro Gersham case."

"No, your birth mom," he said. "Magnolia, Ilia, whatever it was she chose to call herself. When I first ran into her she was a Woodley, you know, her maiden name. And she still had, I don't know, her Earth name, too."

If you missed it earlier in the story, my mother was *very* into *Star Trek* and not at all into lacy, flouncy Southern things. So as soon as she could, she dropped Magnolia as her first name and had her name legally changed to Ilia, the name of a *Star Trek* character. And she was Ilia Woodley until the day she died. She kept her maiden name, though after she married Dad, most people in town insisted on calling her Mrs. Peale.

"I shouldn't bring it up," Graddoch said. "I didn't know her that well or that long, you know. She was just a kid, a really smart and determined kid. I guess that runs in the family."

I leaned forward.

"Now you *have* to tell me more," I said.

Graddoch shrugged, with a charming smile, like a lawyer brushing off the fact that his client was caught with a smoking gun. "Aw, you know, it was just a little tussle about a courtroom Bible," he said.

"What's a courtroom Bible?" I asked.

"Oh, you've never noticed the courtroom Bible because you hardly ever see it," he said. "When people get sworn in to testify in court, they have the option of putting their hand on the Bible to take the oath. Or you can just raise your hand and swear, like someone entering the military. The one time you can really count on people using the Bible for the oath is when they get sworn in as city councilman or sheriff or whatever. Then they want to be in the newspaper with their hand on a big book that's very obviously the Word of God. And the county had a very specific Bible for that purpose. A really worn, floppy old leather Bible that they kept on a little wooden stand in the presiding judge's courtroom over at the county courthouse.

"So, if you get up to testify in that courtroom, you might put your hand on that big book, and swear to tell the whole truth," Graddoch continued. "And the rest of the time, the Bible, you know, it just sits there on a podium in front of the judge's bench. Well, most of the time, anyway, it sits there.

"A Strudwick County jury is, you know, what it is," Graddoch went on. "Select twelve random landowners from this county, Black or white, man or woman, and every man jack of them is going to be a churchgoer, or he's going to claim to be. Sometimes folks would try to get out of jury duty by claiming that they had a conflict because the prosecutor goes to their church. And the judge would always ask, 'but do *you* go to your church?'

"Anyway," Graddoch continued, "With a jury like that, it's just too much to expect a prosecutor, in the throes of a closing argument, not to pick up that Bible, and clutch it to his chest, and invoke the name of Jesus and His stern Father. I mean, the Bible tells us thou shalt not kill, thou shalt not steal. An eye for an eye. How could a prosecutor not wave the Word of God in front of a jury? And if the prosecutor picks up the Bible, any decent defense attorney is going to pick it up in his turn, and talk about forgiveness, and walking a mile in someone else's shoes, even though that's not in the Bible. It's strongly implied. Seventy times seven and all that.

"Well, at one point we got a new presiding judge by the name of Francois Condrey," Graddoch said. "He was 'Pudge' Condrey in high school and law school, but when you put on the robes you have to use the name your mother gave you. Pudge hated this use of the Bible in the courtroom. He thought it was sacrilegious, and he took to warning lawyers not to touch the Good Book during their arguments. But they just couldn't help themselves. No good lawyer could. I mean, if I have to pick up a Bible to keep my client out of jail I'm not going to let fear of God or contempt of court stop me. God will forgive you, and everybody else's decisions can be appealed.

"So one day jury selection begins and somebody notices the Bible is missing. Turns out Judge Pudge had the thing locked away in the court reporter's office, to be brought out only for swearing-in. He'd had enough of this Bible-grabbing. He gave, I hear, a very moving little speech to the lawyers in attendance about respect for the sacred, and about separation of church and state as something that keeps the church clean and the state free.

"Well, that was the end of Pudge Condrey in Strudwick County. The very next day, Liz Deadmon filed to run against him for his judgeship."

"What, like *Senator* Deadmon?" I asked.

"The very same," Graddoch said. "The Flaming Nun herself, the firebrand of the religious right. She who never lost an election. From this courthouse all the way up to the US Senate, if Liz Deadmon wants it, she wins it in a 70-30 vote.

"This was Deadmon's first race as a religious zealot," Graddoch went on. "By Wednesday of that first week she was on religious talk radio saying Judge Condrey had taken the Bible out of the courtroom. Right here in the River City, a judge taking Jesus out of the justice system. It was all hooey, of course, but by Thursday it was on the Birmingham TV stations and by Sunday, Pudge couldn't show his face in his own church.

"The next weekend, there was a big rally right there in the parking lot of the Commission building. Thousands there. Really. Bigger than anything anyone had seen since the Civil Rights movement. And of course, all the politicians who wanted to get into office or stay there, they were all jockeying to get on the stage with Liz Deadmon. Fischer King was there, very young, still had all his hair, was just a high school student president or something. Even then, he knew that if you want to be governor one day, this is a stage you want to be on. Lucy Magby was there. She was already middle-aged, and had already lost a governor bid. Hell, I was there. I had my own political career going. Speaking at that thing was one of the hardest things I've ever had to do. Because, you know, Pudge wasn't a close friend but he was a friend. After I spoke, I slipped out of the rally and went up to the courthouse and found Pudge in his office and told him, you know, that it's all just politics, and nothing personal. And Pudge Condrey was just broken. He wept in a way that was just kind of unmanly. It was shocking.

"I went back over to the rally, which just kept going on and on," Graddoch said. "I was on the edge of the crowd, trying to work my way back in, and I heard all this commotion. Yelling. I saw a bunch of folks kind of standing in a circle, some of them waving their fists. And above their heads I saw a sign on a stick. FREE JUDGE CONDREY, it said.

"So I shoulder my way over there. And what do I see but a little red-headed girl, maybe sixteen years old, holding two signs, arguing with maybe twenty people who were a head or two taller than her. Magnolia Woodley. There was the FREE CONDREY sign and her other sign said THOU SHALT NOT BEAR FALSE WITNESS. She's wearing sort of like a blue miniskirt dress and go-go boots, which was very much not the fashion then, and it threw me off until I realized it was from *Star Trek*. It had the little gold Space Club logo on it."

"Starfleet," I said. "A science officer's uniform."

"Well, anyway, there she was, shouting all kinds of stuff about fairness to Judge Condrey and separation of church and state and the intentions of the Founding Fathers and all that," he said. "What I could hear, over the shouts, sounded very, very intelligent and well-reasoned. Which, I'm sure you realize now, is not the best way to address an angry mob in Alabama.

"At one point, an old lady steps up and literally takes a swing at your mother, using some language one doesn't often hear from a churchgoer. And I could see the look of fear on Magnolia Woodley's face. I don't doubt that if a man had attacked her in the same way, Miss Woodley would have fought back. But you can't hit a bent-over old lady with a sign on a stick. And, you know, once one fist flies it just goes downhill from there. So I stepped in and told everyone to stand back, that this young lady was with me and we were leaving. Everybody knew me. She knew me. I was on political ads on TV all the time. So they let me go. I don't think your mom would have gone with me normally, but she was just stunned.

"When we got free of the crowd she stopped and looked up at me with really serious, steely eyes. 'Why are you here, Backsley Graddoch?' she says. 'You know Liz Deadmon is lying. You know the judge has a right to store that Bible wherever he wants. Why are you going along with this?' Of course, I didn't have an answer—nothing that an idealistic person like you or your mother would understand. So I turned the question back on her. Why are you, a little girl, here all alone?

"And she says, 'Because I couldn't get anyone else to come with me.' Which, you know, is a good answer, I guess. Anyway, Pudge lost everything, his friends, the election. Had to leave town and find work as a divorce lawyer in Mobile. And over the years, I thought that if he had half the guts your mother had, well, let's face it, he would have lost the election and his friends anyway. But he'd still be a man."

"So Liz Deadmon won," I said. "But the Bible's gone now. I mean, I've never seen a Bible on a podium in the courtroom."

"Well, my understanding is your mom played a bit of a role in that," Graddoch said. "A couple of years later, she goes to the court to have her name changed from Magnolia to that *Star Trek* thing. And the case winds up in Deadmon's courtroom. And Deadmon gives her some kind of lecture about how wrong it is to give up your Christian name—you know, that's another word for your first name. She gives a lecture about your Christian name, all the while pointing down at that Bible. And your mom, I'm told, goes right down to the American Civil Liberties Union and tries to get a lawsuit started against Deadmon for making a religious thing out of business that shouldn't be religious."

"I have never heard this," I said.

"I'm not all that surprised," Graddoch said. "Your dad just happened to bring it up once, but it wasn't that big of a thing, because the ACLU didn't take her case. For all the lecturing, Deadmon still let her change her name, so there wasn't really much to argue there. But her case did get the ACLU to look. And they found a bunch of other cases where Deadmon was waving around a Bible and saying strange stuff. Ali Ahmadi—you know, the guy who owns Johnson and Junior's gas station?—he had his name change rejected by Deadmon. Deadmon waved the Bible at him and told him he had to be Clay Johnson Jr. till he dies no matter what his religion was. So he sued, and he won. Got his name changed and got the Bible out of the courtroom. But your mom, as it turns out, got the ball rolling."

"Wow," I said. "I guess I should have expected you to know each other. I mean, it's a small town."

"A lady in a spacesuit is hard to miss," Graddoch said. "And she was always on the square with a sign. The gay rights thing, that was another big issue for her. I've always figured she was straight—I mean, she married your father, and all—and I wondered from time to time why a straight person would go out there, all by herself, protesting for somebody else's rights."

I said it quietly, almost as if talking to myself. "Because no one else would go with her," I said.

Graddoch pulled out a handkerchief and wiped a tear, without taking off his glasses.

"Yes, I guess that's it," he said. "Maybe she was protected, in a way. The way Houmahatchee was back then, if an actual gay person had come out on the square, they might not live to see the dawn. But your mom could say harsh things. People tolerated her, in the meanest sense of the word. They weren't nice to her, but over time you got the sense that no one was going to hurt her. They felt a little bad for her, maybe. She always seemed . . ." He put up his hands and let his voice trail off.

"You almost said 'crazy,'" I said.

"No," Graddoch said. "No, that's not the word I'm looking for. Crazy people do fine here. They have friends. Lonely. Your mom always seemed just desperately, desperately lonely."

CHAPTER NINE

◇

A few weeks later, I got a summons to testify in court. The date: February 14.

"Wow, Valentine's Day," Reagan said when she heard. "Even the World's Smallest Woman couldn't have predicted that."

I was glad to be out of school on Valentine's Day. Let's be honest. This holiday causes more harm than good, and everybody knows it. In elementary school, when everybody goes around class and puts some candy in every other student's Valentine's bag, the joy you get from the whole thing is very mild. Maybe you'll get a candy heart with something truly bizarre written on it—"YOU MY GOLDFISH" or something like that—and you'll chuckle a little. That's the most you get out of it. But there's always that one kid who winds up crying, deeply upset that they didn't get as much candy as someone else or that they didn't get a card from that one person they have a crush on. The pain is worse than the gain. Everybody's known this since the days when Charlie Brown was on TV.

It's even worse when you get older. The whole day is just a big, hot-pink, heart-shaped reminder that you don't have a boyfriend or girlfriend. That's not something you need to be reminded to think about, but somehow the reminder makes it worse. It's like being told that your dad drives a very old, cheap car. Once someone tells you your dad's car is too old, you can't unsee it.

"I wish we could listen to music," I said to Dad, as we drove across the Florida State line, on our way to the court appearance.

"You can listen to music," Dad said. "Just turn on the radio."

"I mean music from my phone," I said. That's how old dad's car is. There's no place to hook up your phone. You can charge your phone, though a little doohickey that Dad plugs into this hole he calls "the cigarette lighter." The car is that old. It's from the times when people had just stopped smoking in their cars and were just about to become addicted to their phones instead.

"We can listen to CDs," Dad said.

"I'm not in the mood for Weezer today," I said. The CD case in Dad's car is a Museum of Old Music, but that museum is more educational than it is entertaining. The Cranberries have only two really good songs, and they're on separate discs.

Radio isn't just great, either. In Florida, just like in Alabama, about half the stations you can pick up are religious—a lot of talk about lions and lambs and swords, or choirs singing about angels bowing down to Jesus.

"What's a diadem?" I asked Dad after we listened to about a minute of one song.

"It's like a crown," Dad said.

"Why does God need a crown?" I said. "He's God."

"Symbolism, I guess," Dad said. "When there were kings running countries, I guess it was kind of a radical thing to say that God was your real king."

There are also a bunch of stations where there's just one guy, in a studio, reading the newspaper and making fun of it and getting mad about stuff that's in the news. Talk radio, they call it.

As we drove though Florida on the morning of Valentine's Day, the talk radio guys were all about Elizabeth and her court case.

"Now get this," said one guy on the radio. "In Cross City today, animal advocates from New York City are going to be in court arguing that an elephant has the same rights as a person. The same rights as a person."

"Well, not the exactly the same rights," I blurted out, as if the guy on the radio could hear me.

"It's just another assault on common sense," Radio Man said. "It's an assault on basic values. I mean, they're saying an elephant has the right to vote. That he could own property. That he is a person under the law just like you or your grandmother."

"That's totally not what this case is about," I said. Dad nodded.

"So you've got to ask yourself," Radio Man continued. "Who pays for this? How can anyone have the time or money to pursue this ridiculous, anti-human stuff? Let me tell you something: there are rich and powerful forces, big money, behind all of these goofball projects. Wherever you see a vegetarian weirdo project, big money isn't far behind. In fact, there are news reports that Sir Guy Burgeon has been seen in Dixie County, and is going to appear in the courtroom today."

"Guy Burgeon?" I said. "The space guy?"

You know Guy Burgeon, right? He played bass guitar for a rock band, then invested his money in a company that makes electronic keyboards. Then his company started doing all kinds of research on music technology. Every time someone uses auto-tune in a song or buys a pair of wireless headphones, Guy Burgeon gets a little bit of money. And I guess he owns a bunch of newspapers in New Zealand and a company that makes electric station wagons and a resort in the Bahamas. But he's most famous for his projects that don't make money. Like his plan to dig a hole all the way to the center of the Earth, just to see what's there. Or Burgeon Voyager, a spaceplane that will take paying passengers up into space for five minutes. Tickets cost a million dollars each.

Radio Man went on and on. He said the case began with an online video of Crying Country Girl—a girl with a strong Southern twang who went on Facebook crying and saying "Who Is Elizabeth?"

"You know somebody probably put her up to that," Radio Man said. "I guarantee you that when all is known, we'll find out that some money changed hands between Guy Burgeon and this crying little girl with the Southern accent."

I couldn't help but laugh. "That can't be me," I said. "I have no country-girl cred. And my Southern accent isn't that bad, is it?"

"No accent is bad," Dad said. "But no, you don't sound all that country to me. Maybe it's the hat. Maybe the hat threw them off."

"I'd love to be country," I said. "But nobody who's really country believes for a minute that I'm country."

Dad switched the channel again, to public radio. The headlines: a new and scary report on global warming, a school shooting in Maine, a blogger in Egypt sentenced to five years in prison just for criticizing his government.

"The world is so messed up," I said. "I can't even save a single elephant without people losing their minds. People are going to look at all these problems and they're going to say: with all this going on, why should we worry about a single elephant? How are we going to fix all this?"

Dad turned off the radio.

"I think you're getting more done than you realize," he said. "We have to work on what's in front of us. Everybody has a little piece of the puzzle to work on."

I was quiet for a minute. I'd heard this speech before, and it had always made me feel better. It's the speech about how I was saving the world one animal at the time and Dad was saving the world one defendant at a time.

"So how's the judge thing going?" I said.

Dad sighed. "I was afraid you'd bring that up," he said. "It's going. I've had lunch with three of the five city council members. That's how they interview you, over lunch. And I have lunch set up with two more. And then, when the current judge retires in about a month, they'll meet and vote on who the new judge will be—me or, apparently, one other person they're having lunch with."

"So, what's your piece of the puzzle at that point?" I said.

"Look, I can still defend clients in county court while working as a judge for the city," he said. "It's only a part-time job. I'm still a defense lawyer."

"I don't think Taleesa's going to see it that way," I said.

"No," he said.

"If you get hired as a judge, will you be able to get a nice car like Backsley Graddoch has?" I asked.

"No," he said. "But I'll be able to fix the plumbing in a hundred-year-old house."

I opened the CD case. "Maybe I'm in the mood for Weezer after all," I said. "It's better than radio."

I sat back and watched Florida get more Florida-like with every mile. More palms and palmettos. More people towing boats. People with front license plates that said NATIVE.

I decided to count license plates. If I see more than ten NATIVE plates before Cross City, I'll see Emory at the trial. If I see more than twenty, he'll want to talk to me after the trial is over. I play little games like that all the time. Toni, my therapist, says it's a sign of anxiety, a sign that you're intensely worried about something that's out of your control.

I counted thirteen Florida Native plates before we got to the courthouse.

▮ ▮ ▮

We were almost late, because we passed right by the Dixie County Courthouse without either of us realizing that a courthouse was what we were seeing. It was a broad one-story building that looked like it might have been a Walmart in a former life. It had a shiny metal roof, which was not something I expected to see. Only when we turned around and retraced our route did we see the word COURTHOUSE on the front of the building.

"Well, I'll be," Dad said. "I thought that was a church, or a bingo hall."

Being a witness didn't work out the way I expected, either. I'm used to being in front of the judge and getting to see everything that's going on. When you're the one testifying, though, they don't let you do that. You sit in a little room with your dad and you wait to be called into the courtroom.

"I wonder if Emory will be there," I said.

"Do you want him to be?" Dad said.

"I don't know," I said, which wasn't really true. I can want all sorts of things that aren't likely to happen. I don't have to tell my dad about all of them.

"Nervous?" Dad asked.

"A little," I said. "It bothers me that I don't know anything about what they're saying in the courtroom now. I'm worried that I'll say something that will mess things up for Elizabeth."

"Don't even worry about that," Dad said. "You're just here to talk about what you've seen. It's Ms. Labisky's job to make the case. Your job is just to tell the truth and only that."

Soon a deputy called me into the courtroom. I've been in courtrooms a lot, but this was a strange experience. First, it was weird that this building, which looked like a bingo hall on the outside, had normal wood-paneled walls on the inside. It all looked just like a courtroom you see on TV, all except for the chairs, which were bright aqua blue, like something a mermaid would have in her house. All twelve of the people in the jury box watched me, some of them looking bored and sleepy, some looking a little amused. The judge at first looked too young to be a judge, with platinum blonde hair and a nice tan, but on a second look you could see that she was one of those older people who just put a lot of care into their looks. In Florida, even the judges look healthy.

They made me swear an oath and then I sat down in the witness stand. Looking out, I could see Dorothy Labisky at one table: she had platinum hair like the judge, but was a little heavier and more pale, with a real school-superintendent vibe about her. At the defense table was a young man in a nice suit and an older man who looked a lot like Emory's brother, Russell. It was Emory's dad, with his lawyer.

I scanned the crowd. Yes, there in the crowd was Russell, also in a suit. And there was Emory, looking handsome and sullen, with the same tousle of sandy hair and wearing a plaid button-up shirt. There was a microphone right in front of me, and I resisted the urge to sigh.

I was so moved by seeing Emory that I almost didn't see the other recognizable face in the courtroom. An old man in a nice suit, but with long straggly hair and a goatee and an earring in one ear, sitting in a crowd of younger people with nice suits and less-wild hair. Sir Guy Burgeon, amateur astronaut and ex-rock-star, sitting right there in the back of the room.

"Miss Peale," Labisky said. "I understand there are some people who call you Colonel Peale. Would you prefer that?"

"I would very much not," I said.

I won't bother you with what came after. Imagine all the stuff I've told you so far. And imagine that, instead of me telling you the whole story, you have to get it out of me by asking questions. *What did you experience at the first night of the Strudwick County Fair?* and so on. It's incredibly boring, but it's all done because the jury doesn't know anything about the case except what they hear from the witnesses, so you wind up telling the story piece by tiny piece.

That storytelling went to some strange places. When she got to the part about my relationship with Emory, Labisky asked a bunch of questions about the bear that he won me that first night at the fair. How big was the bear? Did I see the bear as evidence that Emory and I were in a relationship?

"I don't know what bears mean," I said. "If I did, I think high school would be a lot easier."

People in the jury chuckled.

"Do you still have the bear?" Labisky asked.

"Well, sure," I said.

"Why?" Labisky asked.

I looked at Emory. For an instant, he seemed to be looking at me, hopefully, but when his eyes met mine, he looked down at the floor.

"I've never really thought about that," I said. "I guess I kept it because it reminded me of a good memory, one I want to keep. And anyway, even if I wanted to throw it away, it's too big for the kitchen garbage can. I'd have to set it out on the street next to the garbage, and everybody who drove by and saw it would be sad. So maybe that's what a bear means. It's a memory that you want to keep, but also one that's too big to throw away."

That whole conversation took about a minute, and I was in the witness stand for more than an hour. Still, the bear talk is the part of the trial that stands out most in my mind. I kept bracing for questions about kissing or holding hands with Emory, but nobody asked. I guess a bear is better evidence of a relationship. You can't keep a kiss.

"Did you ever see Emory Mumbford, or Russell Mumbford, or any other member of the Mumbford family use a bullhook to discipline Elizabeth?" Labisky asked.

"I'm sorry," I said. "I don't know what a bullhook is."

"If I may, your honor, I'd like to show Exhibit E," Labisky said to the judge.

"Go ahead," the judge said.

Labisky went to her table and picked up something that looked a bit like a black cane with silver handle. She handed it to me. Up close, you could see that the silver handle-like part wasn't a handle at all. It was a pointy metal tip, one you wouldn't want to be hit with. Suddenly it dawned on me what a bullhook was for.

"Emory!" I blurted out. "Please tell me you're not using this on Elizabeth?"

Emory was still looking down, but his face flushed and his jaw tightened.

"Objection!" the Mumbfords' lawyer shouted.

"Sustained," said the judge. "Ms. Peale, Ms. Labisky, the witness will not address anyone in the audience. Do I make myself clear? Jurors, you're to ignore this outburst."

"Ms. Peale," Labisky said. "Atty. Let's be really clear and factual. Did you ever see anyone use this device on Elizabeth the elephant?"

"I don't think so," I said. "I don't recall seeing something like this."

"Did you see Russell Mumbford using or carrying any sort of stick or pole when he was with Elizabeth?" Labisky said.

I was stunned. "I'm not sure," I said. "I don't really remember. I think maybe so, but I couldn't say for sure."

"Your honor," grumbled the Mumbfords' lawyer.

The judge turned to me. "A simple yes or no will do," the judge said.

"No," I said. "Because I can't say yes for sure, I have to say no."

It was the whole truth and nothing but. In my gut I was sure I saw Russell with some sort of stick, but I couldn't swear to it. I couldn't swear to it because I hadn't been paying attention to those details. I'd been caught up in other things.

The testimony went on. Then it was time for the Mumbfords' lawyer to question me. He stood up and introduced himself politely—Darnell Johnson, Esquire—and even paid a few compliments to my work at the animal shelter. I felt like I barely even heard most of it, because my mind was racing.

I could remember my fortune from the World's Smallest Fortune-Teller. I could remember that the Amazing Celebrity Look-Alike was named Elizabeth Tavoris. And yet I couldn't remember whether or not Russell was holding a weapon he might use to beat an elephant. Was that what the fair was really about? Is the magic all just a distraction, to keep you from seeing the important details?

"Now, let's be clear, Ms. Peale," Johnson said. "You did not know what a bullhook was before today."

"Objection," Labisky said.

"Sustained," said the judge.

"Ms. Peale," Johnson said. "Before today, had you ever heard of a bullhook?"

"No," I said.

"Did you or did you not see a bullhook being used on Elizabeth?" he asked. "A simple yes or no."

"No," I said.

Then came the painful part. For a very long time—maybe it was ten minutes, but it felt like an hour—Johnson asked me the same question in about fifty different ways. Did I get involved with Emory in order to snoop around and collect information on the elephant operation?

"Did you know about the elephant rides when your family decided to come to the fair?" he asked.

"No," I said.

"Did you know about the elephant rides the first time you encountered and spoke to Emory?" he said.

"No," I said.

"Did you continue to have a boyfriend/girlfriend relationship with Emory after you found out you were on opposite sides of this elephant issue?" he asked.

"Well, I tried, I think, but it didn't work out," I said.

"By 'tried' you mean you called him and contacted him," Johnson said.

"Yes," I said.

"And your goal was to continue the relationship?" he said.

"I don't know," I said. "It's like asking what a bear means."

"Counselor," the judge said. "Can we at long last move on from this?"

"Yes, your honor." Johnson slowly paced back to the table and looked at some of his notes.

There was a long pause before he spoke again.

"Ms. Peale," he said. "Is it your impression that Emory loves Elizabeth? That he cares about this elephant?"

"Yes, absolutely," I said.

"How can you then also allege that he's harming this elephant, or that his family, in maintaining this elephant, are doing the animal harm?" Johnson said.

"You're asking me to explain things I can't explain," I said. "I'm learning that people often hurt the people they love. Even when they try, as hard as they can, not to. I'm doing it right now."

I couldn't help but get a little crack in my voice when I said that. Emory covered his face with one hand. Whatever expression was on his face, he wasn't going to share it with me.

"You say we hurt the people we love," Johnson said. "You mean the people and the animals we love."

"To me, animals are people," I said.

Johnson got a gleam in his eye.

"We've established that you're an accomplished animal activist," he said. "Would you say that you agree with the plaintiffs in their belief than an elephant is a person just like a human?"

"Not just like, maybe, but yes," I said.

"So an elephant has a soul, like you and me?" he asked. "An eternal soul that is meaningful to God?"

"I believe that an elephant has a soul like you and me. I don't know whether a soul is eternal, or whether it matters to God."

"So you're an atheist or an agnostic," he asked.

"I'm saying I'm under oath and I'm not going to sit here and say I know something I don't know," I said. "I don't know whether a soul is eternal, and you don't either."

"Do you *believe* a soul is eternal?" he said. "Do you believe that you're going to be in heaven someday, and elephants and dogs and worms are going to be there with you?"

"Counselor," the judge said. "I'm going to ask you to stop hounding Ms. Peale with this line of questioning. It's not badgering, but it's damn silly."

"I'm just trying to establish whether the witness is in the mainstream of beliefs on animal rights," Johnson said.

"Past popes have said you can have your dog in Heaven," the judge said. "I think we can stipulate that the Pope represents a part of the mainstream of religious belief in America."

"I would like to meet my mother in heaven," I said. "I do want Heaven to exist, and I believe that if it does, my mother is there, and I would very much like to go there if only to meet her, because I never really go to know her."

The courtroom went silent. One of the jurors wiped a tear from her eye.

"I'm sorry, your honor," I said. "I didn't mean to blurt out something irrelevant. I just wanted to establish that I'm a normal person. I think wanting to meet your mother, if you've never met her, is normal."

"It's all fine, Miss Peale." The judge turned to the lawyer with a scowl. "Are you quite done with the witness now?"

"We're done, your honor," the lawyer said.

❚ ❚ ❚

"That was bizarre," I told Dad when I got back to the witness waiting room.

"So we're done here?" Dad asked.

"According to the judge, she's free to go," said the deputy in the waiting room. "But just between you and me, if you're curious about the outcome, you might want to hang out a bit."

"Do tell," Dad said.

"Well, you didn't hear it from me," the deputy said, "but when they recessed, the lawyers for both sides went into the judge's chambers, and Guy Burgeon went in there with them."

"Why is Rocket Man even here?" I asked.

"All I know is what I hear," the deputy said. "And I hear there's been a lot of talk between Burgeon and these elephant people about some kind of business deal. Anyway, if you want to hang out for a bit, there are a couple of good places to eat."

Not far from the courthouse, there was one of those restaurants Dad calls a "meat-and-three." You know, where you go through a cafeteria line and they scoop up collard greens and cornbread and that sort of thing and plop it on your plate. For me, I guess, it's just a Three.

"Honey, don't you want no meat?" said the lady at the cash register. "Just potatoes and squash and stuff?"

"I'm good," I said.

I wolfed it down. I was so anxious during the testimony, I hadn't realized how hungry I was getting. I couldn't have been hungrier if I'd been swimming the whole hour. Dad and I didn't talk much. Even I have a limit on how much courtroom stuff I can talk about in a single day.

We walked back to the courthouse to get in the car, and that's when we saw the press conference. A handful of reporters were gathered in front of the courthouse steps. There was a microphone set up at the top of the steps. Guy Burgeon was there, with Emory's dad at his side, getting ready to speak. Dad and I hung out at the back of the crowd.

"Thanks for coming, everyone," Burgeon said. "As you just heard from the judge, I've been in talks with Mumbford Entertainment for several days about the possibility of acquiring Elizabeth and transporting her to my ranch in South Florida. For those of you who aren't familiar with Burgeon Ranch, you may be happy to know that we have two hundred acres of elephant habitat, and there are two other Asian elephants already living there, purchased from circuses. This is all financed by me, personally, so there will be no need for Elizabeth or any of the other elephants there to perform or work or anything like that. Elizabeth has worked a long time with the Mumbford family, and now she'll get to retire and get about the business of being an elephant. And as you know, the judge has dismissed the case now that we've come up with a new living situation for Elizabeth."

"Why now?" asked a reporter. "Why are you coming to this arrangement right when the case comes to court?"

"Honestly," Burgeon said, "I didn't even know about Elizabeth's existence until Miss Peale's video appeared online." He looked me in the eye and nodded a little as he said this, but I don't think any of the reporters in the group even noticed that I was behind them. "I made an offer soon after that. I think it's safe to say that the exact monetary amount was part of the issue. I'll leave it to the Mumbfords to talk about their concerns and their reasons for finally making the decision."

Mr. Mumbford leaned over toward the microphone.

"We have no comment at this time," he said.

"How much did you pay for the elephant?" another reporter asked.

"I don't think we're going to be disclosing that," Burgeon said. "I think it's safe to say that we made it worth the while for the Mumbford family. You have to realize, Elizabeth is the heart of the family business. Mr. Mumbford, I think, is free to disclose the amount if he wants to."

"No comment," Mr. Mumbford said.

Emory was nowhere to be seen. Looking around for him, I caught a glimpse of Dorothy Labisky, wheeling her big briefcase out of the courthouse and through the parking lot to her car. A couple of reporters noticed her, too. They broke off from the press conference and headed toward Labisky. Dad and I trailed behind.

"I think I know what you're going to ask," Labisky said, before anyone asked anything. "I can say this: if, indeed, Mr. Burgeon is willing to maintain Elizabeth under humane conditions, in contact with other elephants, it's a great victory. Obviously we're disappointed that the court isn't going to take up the other major issue here: the question of whether an intelligent animal has some rights. I think most people in this country, if they think about it, really do believe in those rights. It's an issue that's going to have to be decided, at some point, in the courts. The fate of these beautiful, intelligent creatures should be a matter of concern for our government. It shouldn't be left to the whims of a billionaire."

Finally, the reporters noticed me and Dad in their midst.

"How about you, Miss Peale?" one of the reporters asked. "Are you satisfied with the outcome here?"

"I care about all elephants," I said. "But I only *know* one elephant personally. If Elizabeth is happy, it's a win."

I held up my hand, and Dad high-fived me.

▮ ▮ ▮

"Too bad the camera guys weren't there for that part of the interview," Dad said later, in the car. "That high five would have been a great shot."

I chuckled.

"You're just proud you didn't mess it up," I said. "You're the most high-five-missingest dad I know."

"If I had good coordination, I'd be a pilot or something, instead of a lawyer," Dad said.

"I'm not talking about coordination," I said. "I'm talking about a girl holds up her hand and you look at her like you have no idea what she's doing. Look. I'm holding up my hand right now."

"I'm driving," Dad said.

We watched the palm trees and power poles of Florida as they slid by.

"You know," Dad said. "It really is a victory. You can be happy."

"What's that supposed to mean?" I asked.

"I don't know," Dad said. "You just seem a little . . . distracted."

"I can be happy and sad at the same time," I said. "I'm large. I contain multitudes."

"But, really," Dad said, "think of this. You got the ball rolling. Elizabeth lost her family maybe forty years ago. She's lived most of her life without regular contact with another elephant and now, thanks to you, she'll get to run free. Free-ish, at least. She'll get to know other elephants for the first time. She won't be lonely."

Lonely.

"Yeah," I said. "That is good. Really."

"Who knows?" Dad said. "Maybe she'll even, this late in life, find an elephant form of true love."

True love.

"Maybe," I said.

Dad glanced at me for a second.

"Well, look, even if she doesn't find true love, she'll be with other elephants," Dad said. "I mean, as long as you're with other elephants, as long as you have an elephant family, you're never really alone, right?"

I smiled and patted Dad's hand.

"That's right," I said.

It's not like me to smile a fake smile, but sometimes you make the expression and you hope the emotion follows it. And I really was happy for Elizabeth.

But deep down, I knew that true love wasn't quite the same as just being around other elephants.

CHAPTER TEN

◇

Dad didn't become a judge after all.

Just a few days after our trip to Dixie County, Dad had lunch with his fourth council member. Nobody in his first three interviews had any tough legal questions. Nobody on the council was a lawyer. Two of them said they wanted him to be tough on crime, and he told both of them that as a judge his role was to do just what the law asked, no more and no less.

The fourth meeting was with Councilwoman Lena Henderson, the youngest person on the council, and undoubtedly the easiest to talk to. She had a rich, gruff husband who owned a construction company. Lena Henderson and her husband were trying to have a kid but the Lord had not blessed them with that yet, a fact she told to everyone within about five minutes of meeting them. She would overshare like that, but nobody minded because she called everybody "sweetie" and "honey," and not in a mean way. Even kids knew her because she had a loud voice, and because she spent a lot of money at the same shops kids like to go to. In Houmahatchee, everybody goes to Guns and Fudge on the weekend after Thanksgiving because they have a special Christmas train set that runs through the store. Lena Henderson has been at Guns and Fudge probably half the times we've been there, being nice very loudly.

"So I'm at lunch with Lena Henderson," Dad told us, with a twinkle in his eye. "And of course we'd barely sat down when she tells me that she and her husband are trying to have kids, and she asks if I have kids, and then she asks to see them, so I pull up a photo of Atty and Martinez and I hand it to her."

Taleesa shifted in her seat. "I hope this isn't going to be what I think it is."

"Well, she was very . . . sweet," Dad said. "She said, 'Oh it's so kind of you and your wife to adopt a little Black child.' For what's it's worth, she seemed genuinely happy to see a family of people of different races."

"Atty," Martinez said in a high-pitched voice, fluttering his eyelids. "I'm a little Black child. A helpless child."

"Enough, y'all," Taleesa said. "I want to know what you said in response to this, Paul."

"Well, I said the first thing that comes to mind, which is the truth," Dad said. "I told her Atty's my child from a previous marriage and Martinez is my wife's child from a previous marriage."

Taleesa laughed. "Oh, I bet that went over well," she said.

"Oh, she was totally cool," Dad said. "No raised eyebrows or anything. But I could see that she was trying to figure it out. I could tell that she, and maybe the other members of the council, too, had figured I was married to someone . . . I don't know, a little more like Lena Henderson."

"A white lady," Martinez said.

"And, you know," Dad said. "I just decided right then and there that I didn't want to be a judge. The councilwoman didn't do anything wrong, exactly. But suddenly I realized I didn't want to do this. My family's not that complicated. I'm certainly proud of all of y'all. I just don't want to be in a place where I have to explain who I am, or who my family is, or why I don't go to church or any of that. And the bizarre thing is, my clients ask these questions all the time, and they're usually pretty rude about it. I've never minded explaining any kind of thing to them."

"Well, if your lawyer explains something like that to you, you'll remember it," Taleesa said. "Not everybody bothers to remember. Let me tell you, as a Black Wisconsin-born woman in Houmahatchee, Alabama: a lot of people don't remember a lot of things. There are people who've asked me fifteen times if I'm from here or from Montgomery. Explaining is one of the most tiring things you can ask people to do."

And that was it. Dad quietly pulled his name out of the running and everything went back to normal. Because, you know, we are normal. It's normal for a lawyer to drive an old Hyundai that goes clackety-clack, if that lawyer's clients are the poorest people in Strudwick County. It's normal for a kid to have a few grownup friends like Megg and Toni and Backsley Graddoch. It's normal to dress like Batman for a year, because, I mean, who wouldn't do that if their mom would let them? It's normal to have colorful swearing as your main superpower. It's the most common of all the superpowers.

My phone went back to normal, too.

No calls from any interesting boy.

No text messages.

No word from Emory.

I did get an email from Sir Guy Burgeon. He apologized for contacting me directly, and he said his "people" could answer any questions I had about Elizabeth's welfare. He also included a link to a website where anyone can look at live camera feeds from his elephant preserve in Florida.

I'm becoming very familiar with Florida weather. It's humid there, like it is here, and the humidity makes the webcam shots hazy. During the day, the image is a smudgy green. At night all the cameras go nearly black. On a few overcast days, the view is clear and in full color. I check in multiple times every day, and I see the lighting and the color changing, but I don't see a lot of elephants. There's a feeding station, and at mealtimes Elizabeth and her new friends come out to grab some hay. Then they leave, disappearing into the foliage. Being seen by people isn't important to them.

Sometimes a camera catches them going through a clearing on the way to somewhere else. All three elephants together. Sometimes two will be side-by-side, touching trunks. Usually I want to say "hi" to the screen, even though I know they can't hear me, but even this seems like an invasion. They're going about their elephant business.

I don't recall writing back to Burgeon. If I did, it was a simple "thank you, I'll look." Even so, a lot of people in town now think I'm friends with a billionaire. Backsley Graddoch and I completed our twenty-year shelter plan in May, and by June the Strudwick County Commission voted four-to-one to recommend it to the Legislature as a state Constitutional amendment.

"You could have just told us from the start that you were working for Guy Burgeon," said Commissioner Frank Feeney, who cast the only "no" vote. "Simple question, simple answer, we all save time."

I wanted to explain that I don't have anything to do with Guy Burgeon, but Graddoch whispered "no" and shook his head a little. So I held my tongue.

"People can be dumb sometimes," he said. "But as long as everything works out in your favor, maybe it's best not to instruct them. There's some stupid that can't be fixed."

I I I

I guess I'm dumb, too. Not dumb enough to keep wearing a bad hat, but dumb enough to go back to the county fair, a whole year later. The whole family went back.

"Let's try and not let Atty destroy the fair this time around," Martinez said on the car ride to the fairground.

"Hey, you're the one who wanted to sue Fall to Your Death," I said.

Reagan didn't come with us this time. I needed to wander the fair alone, carrying my own tickets and my own memories, at least for a while.

Memory is a sad thing. Whenever I smell hay and waffle-cones, whenever there's a nip in the air and speed-metal competing with carousel music, I'm going to feel the same feelings I felt back then. It's going to be that way from here until the end.

Some parts of the fair had changed. Elizabeth Tavoris was gone, dead or retired or looking like a celebrity in some other town. I rode the Tunnel of Love by myself. I don't know what I was expecting from a love-themed ride, but this one had lots of stops and fast starts and strobing lights, and it felt vaguely like a knock-off of Space Mountain. The theme, I think, is that love feels like being shot out of a cannon in the dark.

Coming out of the Tunnel of Love, I saw a familiar face. Out there in the open, walking around among the crowd, was the World's Smallest Woman. For some reason, I'd never forgotten her face, and she was wearing the same kind of boring mom-clothes she wore when I saw her the year before.

She wasn't that small. She was about the same height as me, which is short for a grownup, but I'm pretty sure the French teacher at Houmahatchee High is about the same size. I couldn't resist saying something when I walked past her.

"Hi," I said.

She looked at me suspiciously. "Do I know you?"

"I think you read my fortune once," I said.

"Ah," she said. "Well, did I get it right?"

"You were close," I said. "Close enough."

"Good," she said. "Do me a favor, hon. There are little kids at the carnival. Don't do anything to ruin the fun."

Yes, it's all mirrors, she was saying. *Keep your mouth shut.*

I chuckled about it, but only after I was out of earshot of her. And I chuckled again as I passed a booth where a young dad was trying to win a bear for his daughter. Then, maybe on purpose or maybe not, I headed back to the corner of the fair where I'd first met Elizabeth.

I was shocked, at first.

Because there, once again, was a corral. And standing in front of the corral, in a safari hat, was Russell Mumbford, with a poorly tucked shirt.

RIDE A CAMEL, read a sign on the corral. Inside the corral, Emory's dad was leading a camel in a broad circle, with two elementary-school kids on its back.

"What happened to the hat?" asked a voice from behind.

Emory was a year taller, a year slimmer, with forearms that were a year more muscular. He still wore his flannel shirt with the sleeves rolled up.

"I didn't expect to see you here," I said.

"I didn't expect to see you here," he said.

"Well, it's Strudwick County," I said. "Why wouldn't I come to the fair?"

He looked, briefly, a little hurt, as if I'd brushed away all that had happened between us. Of course there were reasons not to come to the fair.

"Is there something you want?" he said. "Is that why you're here? Is there something you want to say?"

Oh, yes. Oh, yes there is something I want, something I want to say. But I don't think I can.

Emory glanced over my shoulder. "Look, I can't let Russell see me with you," he said. "I have something *I* want to say. Let's go somewhere else."

Not far away there was a tent without a sign on it, without any sort of attraction inside. Emory pulled open the flap and we went in. In the dim light I could see folding tables, piled with cheap stuffed animals and other fair prizes. And I could see Emory's face, just a few feet from mine.

"Atty, I want you to know something," he said. "I never used a bullhook on Elizabeth. Ever. I would never do that. I want you to know that."

This was the boy I loved.

"I understand," I said. "I hope you know that I meant it when I said that you love Elizabeth. I know you do. I said it under oath. And I said under oath that I love you, too. Emory, now that the case is over, maybe we can—"

"No," he said, with a coldness that made my heart stop. "Love is loyalty. You've got to make choices, Atty. If you love me, you're on my side, and my family's side. Right or wrong."

"I just don't believe that," I said. "My friends, right or wrong. That's what bad people say. That's what the mafia says. That's not how it has to work."

"That's how love works, Atty," he said. "It just is. You have to focus in and love some people. You have to love me. You can't just love everybody, animals and all, just the same."

"But I can be fair to everybody," I said

"No," he said. "No, you can't. If Martinez was starving and all you could give him to eat was meat, you would, wouldn't you? You'd kill an animal to feed your brother if you had to."

"Don't be one of those people," I said. "One of those people who are always setting up these choices. Asking you who you'd throw out of the lifeboat if there wasn't room for everybody. People always set up those questions to show you that we're all evil, but it's putting people in the lifeboat that's evil. It's limiting the choices that's evil."

"Atty, you're the one who limited the choices here," he said. "You helped the people who sued my family. You made the lifeboat smaller."

"And now I'm the one you'd kick off the lifeboat," I said. "I'm the one you'd let drown."

Now something changed in his face. A look of angry determination, like I get in court sometimes when somebody says something stupid and suddenly I realize again that, yes, my cause is just.

"You were never in my lifeboat, Atty," he said. "You're just some pretty girl I kissed at the fair. I asked you to be more, but you didn't want that."

Now I was crying, so hard I could barely breathe.

"I want on the boat," I said. "I'm drowning."

"You're not drowning," he said. "You're just sad. You made choices, and now you're sad."

He left. I stood there for a long time, crying so hard I was nearly dizzy. Finally I caught my breath a little.

"I'm drowning," I said, to no one, because I was alone. "Help me. I am. I'm drowning."

In the distance, I could hear the mix of carnival music and heavy metal, and the sounds of happy people laughing.

▮ ▮ ▮

"He really said you were the *pretty* girl he kissed at the fair?" Reagan asked me at lunch the next day. "Well at least you've got that. You're a pretty girl. He was totally mad at you and he said that. An unforced pretty."

I laughed between sobs and wiped my nose.

"You're just saying that to make me feel better," I said. "You hear 'pretty' all the time."

Reagan sighed. "No," she said. "No, not really. I get 'hot' and 'interesting' and 'crazy' and 'sexy,' but guys don't tell me I'm pretty. Guys who are mad at me don't give me compliments."

I sniffled.

"Well, I think you're pretty," I said.

"I know," Reagan grumbled.

I threw my snot-filled Kleenex at her. "To hell with you, Han Solo," I said.

I grabbed another tissue. We sat there for a while without saying anything. It wasn't a tense silence. But it felt like there were all kinds of things just bursting out. Neither of us spoke because all the things we wanted to say were bubbling up to the top, waiting to be said first.

"He's right about you, you know," Reagan said finally.

I smiled. "So you think I'm pretty," I said.

"No, he's right about having to choose," she said. "He's right about picking somebody and sticking with them even when they're wrong. If you're gonna have love, you're going have to pick. One person. You gotta choose between a man or a woman."

"Biphobic," I said.

"No, no, no," she said. "I just mean you've got to pick one. One person. Even if you had two lovers, you'd like one better. All of God's pairs are lopsided. One ear's bigger than the other. One nostril's bigger than the other. And when you pick someone, you stick with them even when they're wrong."

I huffed out a really loud, snotty sigh.

"Augh," I said. "I'm so sick of crying."

"Crying's what you do because you're turning into a damn girl," Reagan said. "That's all the ladies do, is cry, every time they take a lov-ah."

"Lov-ah!" I said.

"Lov-ah!" Reagan said.

Toni the therapist says crying is our secret weapon in the war for mental health. You cry, you feel better. And if you don't feel better, cry again.

I even cried in front of Backsley Graddoch at one point, which was embarrassing. He wanted to console me, I think, but he doesn't hug and he doesn't have any advice for people on breakups. Apparently he's never been through one.

"I'm not good at this," he said. "You know, my lovely bride and I have been married for thirty years."

"What's the trick?" I said, through sniffles. "How do you stay together like that?"

"Oh, it's all a bunch of compromises," he said. "If you love somebody, you wind up giving up all other kinds of things you care about. Everything: a car, a hobby, the color you wanted to paint the house. I think *your* trouble is that you're a very principled person, more principled than me. There are things you won't compromise on. Life's a lot easier if you have fewer principles."

I shook my head. "I don't think that's the answer," I said.

"Well, not for you," he said. "You're Ilia Woodley's daughter."

"Is it too much to ask for someone who loves me, who wants to be with me, who looks into my eyes with love and who stands by me when I stand on principle?" I said.

"If that's the kind of love you want, then I guess it's good you have a dog," Graddoch said.

And he's right, you know. It is good to have a dog.

When I'm gone, Easy lies on the floor in front of the door, waiting for me to come home. I'm told he howls sometimes, if I come home too late. And he howls with me when I play the drums in the garage.

I'm glad Easy was there the last time I cried about Emory. This was a few weeks after the fair. I was at home doing homework, with Easy nudging me for attention, when I felt another wave of loneliness wash over me.

"Let's do this," I said to myself, putting down my pen.

I went to the bedroom and plopped down on the bed and decided I'd just cry as much as I want to. And I did cry, staring up at the ceiling, with Easy snuggling up right next to me, looking confused. I don't know how long I was there, but the light on the ceiling was bright when I started, and it was shadowy when I finished.

I cried until I didn't have any more in me. Until I felt stupid for crying about a boy.

"I think I'm ready to be with other elephants now," I said.

And I was. I was a girl with lots to do. I had a family, and a couple of really good human friends, and I had a dog. That's more than enough to keep a girl happy while she looks for that other thing, that other kind of relationship she craves. Whatever you want to call it.

"Lov-ah!" I whispered to Easy.
But, of course, he couldn't whisper back.
He just looked at me and sighed.

"Leave them alone in the wild"

A CONVERSATION WITH ANIMAL LAW EXPERT KATHERINE MEYER

Katherine Meyer is a real-life, grown-up Atticus Peale.

Meyer is the director of the Animal Law and Policy Clinic at Harvard Law School. The clinic teaches law students about animal law—basically, all the aspects of law that apply to nonhuman animals—while also weighing in on important cases that affect animal welfare.

She didn't start out as an animal lawyer. Soon after she graduated from law school, Meyer went to work for various public interest groups—the Center for Auto Safety, the Freedom of Information Clearinghouse and the Public Citizen Litigation Group—taking on court cases to help improve the safety of cars and to enforce government rules on food and drug safety, among other things.

In 1993, she founded Meyer & Glitzenstein, a law firm that takes on cases on behalf of nonprofit groups. Soon she was working on behalf of animal welfare groups, taking legal action to stop public pigeon-shooting events, to protect wild horses in western states, and to get better protection under the law for captive chimpanzees. She's probably best known for taking on Ringling Brothers, the circus that, for decades, traveled the country with performing elephants as part of its show. Meyer argued that elephant training harmed the elephants in a way that violated the Endangered Species Act. After the case brought more public attention to harmful practices at the circus, Ringling Brothers stopped using elephants in its show and released its elephants to sanctuaries.

Like Atty, Meyer often struggles with the issue of "standing," the notion that someone must have something at stake in an issue before they can take that issue to court. Animals can't file lawsuits on their own behalf, and if a person is going to file a suit to defend an animal, that person has to show the court why they have an interest in the animal's welfare.

She's perhaps the nation's foremost expert on animal law relating to elephants. When I approached her as part of my research for *Atty in Love*, she graciously agreed to sit for an interview to discuss her own career in animal law and to talk about how young people can make their world a kinder place for animals.

I I I

Tell me a little about how you got involved in animal law.

I got into animal law because I've always loved animals, and I've always loved nature, and I was a public interest lawyer. I was doing mostly consumer protection law. But I had learned about how to use the law to fight for what's right, and I started bringing cases that I thought were necessary to help protect animals.

I brought cases to protect the bison in Yellowstone National Park, and live birds used at shooting events in various states, and primates in zoos and primates in research. I just started bringing lawsuits on behalf of my clients. Once we won one lawsuit, other groups would come to us with their issues and ask us if we could help them fashion a legal remedy or a legal strategy for protecting a particular animal.

What's the biggest challenge in pursuing these cases?

The biggest challenge, I would say, is to be able to establish standing on behalf of a human being who wants to protect animals. That's the biggest challenge, and the second biggest challenge is the resources that are required. You've got to have a lot of money to bring these cases, mainly because they involve procuring experts who can testify on your behalf, and to explain to the judge how these acts that you may be challenging harm the elephants, or harm any animal. You have to have some expert testimony, and experts, that's what they do for a living. You have to pay them for their time, usually. So I would say that establishing standing and having the resources to see these cases through to the end are the most challenging things about them.

You've sued circuses to try and get their performing elephants into more humane conditions. When an elephant is living under humane conditions, what does that look like?

The really, truly only humane conditions are leaving them alone in the wild. They need a huge amount of space.

They travel hundreds of miles every year. That's what they do. They need to be with others of their species. They are incredibly social animals. They need to be with each other. They need to stay with their young. In circuses and in other kinds of "entertainment" using animals, they often separate the babies from their mothers and hand-rear them, so they can control them. That's just devastating to an elephant. Like humans, they're extremely social beings, they're intelligent, they need lots of space and they need others of their species, and they need to be left alone. They need to be able to engage in their natural behaviors. They need access to water—they're swimmers, and they bathe themselves in mud. You really can't keep an elephant in a "humane" captive setting. It's very difficult.

Now, there are sanctuaries that try to mimic those natural conditions as much as possible, for elephants who were saved. Obviously these animals can't go back to the wild, even if they were taken from the wild originally, they're not able to go back, so there are sanctuaries that try to mimic as much as possible those conditions, and give them space and enough elephants to hang out and play with, and enough water to swim in and mud to bathe in, and so on—but it's really very difficult because they're so huge, and they really do require a lot of habitat.

What can a kid—let's say a kid in middle school or the early high school years—do to help with this issue and with animal rights generally?

I think the most important thing is to become educated, and I think that someone who wants to help animals will be motivated to do so. Find your passion and what you're interested in—maybe it's a particular species, maybe it's a particular area of the world, maybe it's a practice you don't like—and just learn everything you can about it. With the internet, that's pretty easy.

Learn everything you can, and then find out what organizations are engaged in the kinds of advocacy that interest you and volunteer. Find out what they do. Follow what you can do to help them.

If you want to take it to the next level, when you get out of high school, go to college, get as much education as you can in biology or wildlife protection or environmental law, whatever it may be. Design your curriculum to further your education in these issues. And then, if you want to be able to go into animal legal work and do something about these practices, go to law school.

If someone's in middle or high school and they want to go to law school eventually, what would you advise them to do right now?

I would advise them to do something that would demonstrate that they really have a passion for this field, so that, by the time they're ready to go to law school, they can show the law school—and particularly law schools that have robust animal law programs—that this is what they want to do in life, as demonstrated by a documented record of becoming educated in this field and volunteering their time. That will go a long way, though obviously you have to have good grades. But actually being able to demonstrate that this is what you care about, that's something that a law school that has a good animal law program, like Harvard, would look kindly on.

To me, that's what I'd want to see on a resume: that it's not just for show, and that you really care about animals and want to use your talents to do so.

Acknowledgments

This book wouldn't have been possible without the help of a many kind people, and they deserve some thanks.

First, I'm grateful to Katherine Meyer, who really is the country's top expert on exactly the sort of activism Atty does. She graciously gave me her time for an interview, and that interview helped me know where I was on the right track and where I needed to change course.

Seven Stories Press editor Tal Mancini poked and prodded this manuscript and found dozens of places where a middle-aged author's voice and Atty's progressive spirit didn't quite match. Of my three books, this was the hardest to edit, and I'm glad I was in such capable hands.

The English Department at Jacksonville State University felt like home to me even before I was hired to teach there, and I find it a very humane workplace for anyone who wants to write. Anytime I asked for help, I got it.

My biggest thanks belong to readers, particularly the middle-school and high-school kids who responded to the first book. At one school visit, a young reader came to me and begged me to tell her that Reagan was gay. I told her what you now know: Reagan is straight, but there is an LGBT character in *Atty at Law*, and the clues are there if you look. In our current climate—with gay authors getting disinvited from school visits, and LGBT-themed books pulled off the shelves—I knew there was some risk in having Atty reveal this now, but I drew a lot of courage from the knowledge that there was at least one reader out there who wanted to see Atty as she is. I'm sure it took some courage to ask. Often, when we are courageous, we get results.

Another courageous young reader asked me to make her a character in my next book. Done and done. I'm sure the real Fallon has plenty of friends, but I should note that the friend mentioned in this book—the one who's not entirely nice to Martinez—is an entirely fictional character.

TIM LOCKETTE is a teacher, writer, and former journalist who lives in Jacksonville, Alabama. His middle-grade debut novel, *Atty at Law*, was praised in a starred review from *Kirkus*. His next two novels, *Tell It True* and *Atty in Love*, were written for young adult readers. *Tell It True* was a Junior Literary Guild Selection and won the Whippoorwill Book Award, which honors books that dispel stereotypes about young people in rural areas and small towns.